Treaty Brides

THE SIEGE BRIDE

SAMANTHA CAYTO

The Siege Bride

ISBN # 978-1-80250-587-0

©Copyright Samantha Cayto 2024

Cover Art by Kelly Martin ©Copyright January 2024

Interior text design by Claire Siemaszkiewicz

Pride Publishing

Published in 2024 by Pride Publishing, United Kingdom.

Collections
Rules of Summer: In the Heat of the Dungeon
Dark and Deadly: Dream Demon
S.W.A.L.K.: His True Heart
His Harem: Room for Elijah

THE SIEGE
BRIDE

Chapter One

The first slap of wind heralding the impending winter made Baron Henry Roth's eyes water. It made peering through his spyglass at the impenetrable fortress looming high above his camp even more irritating than it had already become. Nothing had changed in the weeks since he'd arrived, and he was no further along in his mission of breaching the place. Every day had become the same as the last, with no end in sight.

He suppressed the desire to sigh. "Highrock is certainly well-named."

Sir Colin Beaumont, one of the few men in Moorcondia taller than Henry, leaned his elbow on Henry's shoulder. "This is what comes of you being so good at your job, Hal. The king has sent you here because he believes you are the best man to get in there and stop this rebellion. You have only yourself to blame."

Now Henry did sigh as he lowered the spyglass. "You're right, of course. But not even my prodigious mind for warfare can see a way to take that place without tremendous loss of life. I will not use the bodies of our dead men as a bridge to the gate. The siege must continue, even though it means wintering here."

"Freezing our balls off." Colin took the spyglass and looked through it himself. "How long do you think they can last up there?"

Henry had done the calculations the previous night with the information he had. "I think they can last until spring, actually...maybe longer. Cragmore has been planning this move for a long time, I'll wager, and has filled his fortress with as many provisions as that massive place can hold. Their wells ensure a plentiful supply of fresh water, so running out of food will be the only thing to bring him to heel. I don't think he's going to risk his people starving to keep this ill-gotten autonomy."

Colin snorted as he lowered the glass. "King of the North Cliffs. What nonsense. His ancestor was critical to bringing the disparate factions under the one rule of Moorcondia. This land has prospered ever since. What madness has driven him to declare autonomy, do you think?"

Henry had pondered that very question many times and still had no answer. There was rumor of the old duke losing his senses with age. That, plus the death of his older son, may have been what had tipped his mind into madness—all which was purely speculation. The old guy might simply be a greedy bastard who thought the distraction of fighting the Swarm had made Moorcondia subject to this kind of rebellion. No matter. The king wasn't going to allow Cragmore to break away into a separate country, regardless of how little strategic value the place had. Sedition was something that spread if it wasn't eradicated.

He turned to look at his camp, a sea of tents with thousands of soldiers milling about. They had the advantage militarily but for the impregnable fortress sitting high up on three sides and with sheer cliffs on the fourth one. If they could only get inside, the fight would be swift and hopefully with as little bloodshed as possible. Even if Henry weren't inclined to mercy himself, the king had made it clear — "*Bring the people of Highrock back into the fold. Don't slaughter them.*"

He started threading his way through the camp to his own tent. "Tell the quartermaster we must make plans to provision us through the winter, at least. I assume much of what we'll need will have to be transported to us. The locals can't supply us for much longer, and that's assuming they will continue to want to."

So far, the Cragmore residents had met his arrival with the type of indifference that came from being under someone else's control. Powerful people ruled their lives, regardless of what they thought, and as long as no one was sacking their town and homes, they went about their business, ignoring the nonsense of the ruling class — not that he could be sure no spies or saboteurs mingled among them. It was a near certainty that some of them were personally loyal to the duke.

Colin walked beside him, always a reliable bannerman and as close to a brother as a friend could be. "One thing we won't have to worry about is having enough wine."

Henry glanced up at the only other prominent building in the area. "Ah yes, the good sisters." Honoria Abbey had been in the North longer than the duke's family. The fertile land covering their hills produced excellent grapes, and the nuns living there made exquisite wine. "I assume their reverend mother has kept them apolitical."

"As far as we can tell. They are certainly quick with a smile whenever I encounter one in town."

"Hmm. I don't trust religious types overly much, as you know. We should be extra-vigilant, as the only women in the world who can disarm men easily, other than whores, are nuns. A smiling woman is the greatest weapon to use against a man."

"We are terribly dumb creatures," Colin agreed.

"Ruled by our cocks and stomachs and made vulnerable by our inflated confidence. If we have to remain in this soon-to-be frozen field of mud, we must be careful not to give the duke any information that can strengthen his position. He has the strategic advantage of his location, but we have time on our hands."

"And idleness is the worst enemy for soldiers. I'll remain vigilant. Never fear, Hal."

Henry clapped his friend's back. "I have no doubt, and if we must linger in this place, we at least have each other for company." He didn't elaborate, because Colin understood. Throughout long campaigns, they would spend hours talking, playing chess and also giving each other pleasure. It was a casual thing between them, especially as Colin planned on marrying and fathering children at some point when he was ready to give up soldiering, while Henry had no such interest. He just liked having his needs tended to on a regular basis and disliked using whorehouses. The boys there were often under the duress of having no other options in life, and Henry didn't like preying on others—and neither did his friend. A quick hand or blow job with Colin was the best solution. It was a way of relieving stress without worrying about pressuring those under their command.

Colin cleared his throat. "All this talk of wine has made me thirsty. Shall we retire to your tent for a cup or two?"

Henry was about to agree when a woman's strident voice caught his attention. He turned his head toward the edge of the camp where a road out of town was located. "What's that?" He changed course to investigate.

The guards tasked with guarding who came in and out of town were clustered around a wagon filled with casks. Three nuns stood to one side while a fourth one was giving the sergeant the cutting edge of her tongue.

"You have no right to impede our journey. We have a delivery to make."

The older man, well-used to dealing with difficult encounters of this kind, was clearly trying to keep his temper. "Holy sister, my job is to keep the people of the North here, where they belong. We can't have the enemies of the king wandering about the country, now can we?"

The woman lifted her chin, her green wimple fluttering in the wind. "My good man, surely you aren't suggesting that we sisters are soldiers or spies? We make wine and this," she added with a wave at the wagon, "is an order for our customer in the valley. We only ask to deliver it. I assure you we will return to our abbey within a few days. And," she went on with a very un-nun-like sneer, "we shall *not* be slitting your throats while you sleep when we do so."

The guard tried for affable. "Of course not, madam. But a simple solution is to sell your casks to us. We are happy to buy them from you, and our coin is as good as anyone else's."

"Oh, so now you demand that we renege on our order to a long-standing customer? You'll buy our wine I'm sure for so long as you're here. By the time you're gone, the people outside of the North will have found other suppliers. Is your remit from the king to destroy the abbey's economy?"

This situation had taken a dark turn. Henry hurried to intervene. "What is all this?"

His arrival obviously relieved the guard. He tipped his helmet. "My lord."

The nun turned her gaze on him, her eyes brimming with fury. "You are Baron Roth?"

Henry sketched a bow. "I am."

"Then tell your men to let us pass. We merely mean to go about our business, regardless of your ridiculous dispute with the duke. It has nothing to do with us. My sisters and I are harmless."

Henry doubted that was entirely true. He had a feeling that this nun would stick a knife in one's belly if provoked. The other three were meeker, their heads bowed and hands clasped in front of them. There was very little visible, as was always the case with nuns, being dressed as they were with wimples, long robes and loose belts. They appeared younger than their spokeswoman. The one in the middle in particular had creamy skin that looked as if it didn't get much sun. Now, that was interesting. The others' faces were more golden, as were their hands. Their necks were covered tightly, and while two of them sported slender columns that led into their habits, the middle one's throat looked a little thicker.

Henry trusted his gut. It had saved his life on occasion. At the moment, it was telling him that something was wrong. He approached the three nuns and peered at them more closely. The slight stiffening in all four women told him he was on to something. He ran his gaze down the middle nun, noting her larger hands and how the boots peeking out from the hem of the habit were of excellent quality compared to the others. As he reached the nun and stared hard at her, the woman lifted her face and peered back at him with vivid blue eyes. There was some trepidation in that gaze but also defiance and the kind of haughtiness that was bred into nobility.

Knowing he took a risk that would only enrage the local population, Henry listened to his gut and yanked the wimple off the nun's head. A cascade of silky blond hair, so pale it was nearly white, tumbled out, and the Adam's apple he'd been sure lay behind the cloth was exposed.

Henry was struck dumb for a moment, the boy's beauty that arresting. When he'd recovered his wits, he let a slow smile spread across his face. "Well, well, who do we have here?"

Kellen of Cragmore tightened his grip to keep the trembling from showing. He'd known this idea had been a foolish risk. He should have stayed hidden in the abbey instead of letting the reverend mother talk him into this mad scheme to spirit him away to his mother's people in the South. And he would have resisted more if he hadn't also been afraid that the king's men would somehow discover him and punish the nuns for harboring the son of a traitor who had picked a fight he couldn't possibly win. Now, the good women, who had been nothing but kind to him, were in trouble anyway.

He lifted his chin and glared with more bravado than he felt into the dark eyes of the fearsome Baron Roth. The man had a reputation of being a consummate soldier, and seeing him up close with his short black hair, square jaw and towering height, he could believe everything he'd ever heard about the man. But his reputation included being fair. Kellen could reason with him. He had to.

"I am Kellen of Cragmore."

Roth raised one eyebrow. "The duke's surviving son. How intriguing. What are you doing dressed as a nun and sneaking past my siege?"

Kellen licked his lips, trying to marshal his answer. He didn't miss the way the baron's gaze tracked his movements. And the look in his eyes — hungry — was something he was used to seeing, too. Usually that kind of interest from a powerful man made him afraid. Somehow, though, that wasn't happening this time. If anything, he felt...intrigued. And if he were bold enough, that kind of lust could be used against a man. The trouble was, Kellen had never been daring in his life.

"I was at the abbey when you arrived. They were only trying to keep me safe." He stiffened his spine and gave the baron as fierce a look as he could manage, given that he barely reached the man's chest. "You will not punish them for this. They have nothing to do with my father's plans and acted only out of concern for me."

Roth's expression turned thoughtful. "What were you doing at the abbey?"

Before Kellen could answer, Sister Winnifred stepped toward them. "Leave him be. Kellen is a good boy, only interested in winemaking. He spends most of his days with us, has nothing to do with his father's perfidy and is no danger to you."

"I'm not so sure about that," the baron murmured, his intense gaze making Kellen shake again. "His presence is…disturbing." Then the man smiled at him.

Kellen nearly took a step back from the scrutiny, except there was nowhere to go, and one thing he'd learned in life about powerful men was to never let them see your fear. "I am of no consequence. With my brother's death, my sister has become my father's heir. She sits up there with him," he added with a jut of his chin in the direction of Highrock. "I'm not part of their effort to leave Moorcondia. I doubt they've even noticed I'm not in the castle." That was sadly true. He was so unlike the rest of his family that they'd ceased to pay any attention to him.

A terrifying thought occurred to him. "They won't surrender to save me, either. I can't be used to your advantage."

The baron chuckled as he shook his head, the low timber of his voice skittering along Kellen's skin. "I'm not going to strap you to a catapult and threaten to send you over the wall if they don't open the gates. That doesn't mean, however, that you don't have your uses. I can think of a few already." His tone implied something that was menacing on a level that had nothing to do with warfare.

The baron turned on his heels to face Sister Winnifred. "You may continue on your way, madam. But I hope you will also sell us your most excellent wine. It's going to be a long winter."

The nun's lips thinned. "By the grace of the gods, we serve all people as best we can. You will have your wine, my lord, like any good customer. But you will hand the boy back to us, as well. We'll make sure he stays in the abbey and out of your way."

Kellen had to blink back sudden tears at how this woman was defying a dangerous man on his behalf, even as he knew she wasn't going to get her way. "It's all right, sister. You've all been very kind to me, but I must go with the baron. My birthright ensures that I become a political prisoner. There's nothing either of us can do about that, and I want you all to be safe. It will give me peace of mind. Please."

Before the woman could respond, Roth intervened. "Madam, I give you my word that I won't harm a hair on his beautiful head. I simply can't let him go, though. However he feels about his father's actions, as the man's son, he can become a person for sympathizers to rally around, whether he wants to be or not. He's actually safer with me than he would be out in the world."

Kellen knew the baron was right, although as far as Kellen was concerned, there was no safe place for him. The moment his father and sister had openly rebelled against the king, they'd sealed his fate. He would never be free again...not really. He shot Winnifred an imploring look.

The nun gave a curt nod. "I shall do as asked, because I obviously have no choice. May the gods be with you, Kellen." She smiled at him before glaring at the baron. "And may the gods shrivel your manhood if you break your word."

Roth held out his hands. "I assure you, madam, I want no trouble from your good self or the gods. Safe travels." Then he took Kellen by the elbow, his touch firm, yet not painful. "Let's go to my tent and have a little talk, shall we?"

Kellen had no choice but to stumble along, trying to match the man's long strides. With them came a knight who was even taller than the baron, although not as broad or thickly muscled. As they made their way, soldiers gaped at him openly. They didn't jeer at him, a mark of respect, he thought, for their commander. In fact, the looks on the men's faces were that of respect and even affection—if one could ascribe such a sentiment to hardened fighters. Roth was in full command of his men, obviously, and that allayed Kellen's fear that the siege would cause great trouble in town from bored men spoiling for a fight.

It was no surprise when they entered the biggest tent in the camp. Inside was a luxurious place that made even Highrock look shabby. War he might be fighting, but the baron was going to spend the siege walking on plush carpets and sleeping in a large bed sitting on a platform. There was a desk and a few chairs, a low table and tall cupboards for clothing. The baron was dressed plainly in all black, with leather pants that hugged his thick thighs, shiny boots up to his knees and a tunic straining from his broad chest. His belt held a big scabbard with a long sword sporting a simple hilt. No jewels flashed on it the way his brother's had.

The man led Kellen to a chair by a fire pit located under an opening to let smoke out. It wasn't lit, not yet, but it would be soon, given the harsh winter that was coming. "Make yourself comfortable, my lord."

Kellen had no choice, and besides, he was happy to give his shaky knees a rest. He pulled the wimple completely off and ran his fingers through his hair. He watched the men as they spoke with one another.

"Shall I secure a tent to hold our guest, Hal?"

Kellen blinked at the familiar address, then studied the way the men stood close to each other and at their expressions. *They are lovers.* For some reason, the thought disappointed him. *Don't be ridiculous.*

Roth gave him the side-eyes. "That won't be necessary, Colin, but see if my page can rustle up more suitable clothes for the boy. As fetching as he is in even a simple nun's habit, I'd see him dressed in a manner suitable for his station."

"As you say, my lord." Before the knight left, he winked at Kellen. "Our time here has just gotten more interesting—for one of us, anyway."

Kellen was still trying to decipher what the man meant by that when the baron came over and threw himself into the nearby chair. He stretched out his impossibly long legs and clasped his hands on his lap—the perfect picture of a man at ease. "So, Lord Kellen, you like making wine, do you?"

Kellen wanted to refuse to answer, but that wouldn't accomplish anything, and he didn't want to aggravate the man for fear he might take it out on the nuns after all. "I do."

"Why?"

Now he was confused. He'd expected to be peppered with questions about the strategic strengths of his father's castle. This line of questioning befuddled him. Perhaps the baron wasn't as smart a soldier as his reputation implied.

Kellen shrugged. "It's interesting, that's all. The soil here grows wonderful grapes that with patience and effort produce a wine that is full-bodied and fruity without being overly sweet. It keeps me occupied, in any event. Highrock will never be mine, and I have no aptitude for soldiering."

"No indeed, you are too delicate for battle — at least the kind waged by soldiers."

Kellen frowned at that cryptic remark, although the heated gaze the baron sent his way made his cheeks hot. He looked elsewhere to break the connection. "What do you intend to do with me if you aren't going to lock me up in another tent?" The idea that he might be put on display in a cage in the open drained the blood from his face.

"Oh that's an easy question to answer. You're going to stay here...with me."

Kellen whipped his head around. "What? Your tent is big, Baron, I'll grant you that, but it hardly contains space for two to occupy while giving each other room. And you must confer with your men in here. Surely you don't want me to privy to your strategies." His heartbeat ticked up, although whether it was from fear or something else — something entirely inappropriate — he didn't know.

The baron crossed his ankles and slouched even more in his chair. "I'm not worried about any of that, my lord. You'll never be able to help your father with whatever you hear, if for no other reason than he's not letting anyone in. Not even for his own son would he risk lowering his drawbridge. We're stuck with each other for the remainder of this siege, I'm afraid." He waved his hand. "Well, I'm not disappointed about that."

To quell his renewed shaking, Kellen crossed his arms. "You'll get nothing useful out of me. I'll be a pointless irritant for so long as you keep me prisoner in here, underfoot at every turn. You'll probably trip over me when you get up in the morning, because I tend to sprawl when I sleep." He hadn't meant to raise such an intimate subject as his sleeping habits, but the words were out and there was no taking them back.

The baron's response sent a chill up his spine.

Roth threw his head back and laughed, then said, "My dear Lord Kellen, I'm not worried about tripping over you because you won't be sleeping on the floor. You'll be sharing my bed."

Chapter Two

Henry found himself distracted as he listened to the reports of his war council. As he sat at the head of his table, half of his attention kept being drawn to the other side of his tent where his *guest* was putting on the clothing his squire had managed to scrounge up somewhere. The garments were plain, yet worthy of a nobleman, and Kellen was donning them without complaint. Gone was the nun's habit, leaving more than a flash of a slender, toned body with creamy white skin. Really, it was more of a temptation than a man could resist, and Henry wasn't the only one sliding his gaze over to the boy. Those men sitting with the right view were doing so as well. A spurt of annoyance caught him by surprise, and a growl of warning was halfway passed his lips before he stopped it. Colin's smirk from across the table told him he wasn't quick enough off the mark as he should have been.

This possessiveness is beneath me. He's a prisoner, nothing more.

He refocused his attention on the meeting, trying to block out the boy's low voice as he talked with Frederic. The young nobleman's politeness to the squire spoke well of him. Henry had racked his brains for what he knew of the duke's youngest child, and he'd come up with damn little. The older siblings — the dead heir who had broken his neck riding recklessly, according to rumor, and the current one who was known for her bloodthirstiness — had been well-described in the briefing the king's ministers had given him. All that anyone had said about this youngest child was that he seemed to be of no consequence to his father whatsoever. *Practically a ghost, rarely seen and never spoken of.* That had been the description, and it flummoxed Henry. While it was obvious the boy was ill-suited to being a soldier, it was also surprising that someone of such exquisite beauty melted into the background. If Henry had walked into a room filled with a thousand people, his gaze would still have been drawn to this young man.

"My lord?"

Henry blinked at Sir Robert Godfrey, his best tactician. Obviously he'd missed something the man had said. "Sorry. I was wool-gathering. Please repeat what you said?" He shot a glare down the table when Colin chuckled.

Sir Robert, being a man of some considerable age and a consummate soldier, ignored the noise and acted as if he had to repeat himself to Henry every day. "I was saying, my lord, the scouting party I sent to explore the cliffs on the far side have confirmed that only birds are getting in and out of the castle that way."

"Hmm, not surprising, really, although I find it hard to believe that there isn't an escape route out of the place. If it were my home, I'd have one. Actually, my home does have one," he amended, thinking of the tunnel deep beneath the family home. As children, he and his brothers had loved playing in it. He turned to eye Kellen, who now sat back in the visitor's chair, fully clothed as a boy. "I'm keen to know more about the layout of the fortress and may have an opportunity to glean its secrets."

Hugh of Farley leaned forward. "As your security chief, I don't much like the idea of that lad staying in your tent, my lord. I can tuck him up nice and tight in another tent and bring him here any time you want to interrogate him."

Henry couldn't hold back a smile. "You're not seriously worried that boy is any danger to me?"

Hugh scratched his stubbly chin. "Even a child is dangerous if they get close enough with a weapon. I can't see the point in taking the risk."

It was on the tip of his tongue for Henry to snap out that his man was being ridiculous, and it was none of his concern. But he was right about the danger, and being the head of security for the entire camp, this was exactly his business. "You make a fair point, Hugh, and I respect your counsel on this. Nevertheless, Lord Kellen stays here. I want my eye on him, and he might prove more useful if he's comfortable," he added in a low voice. Kellen wasn't so far away that he couldn't catch most of what they were saying.

When he glanced in the boy's direction, he was met with a glare. The Cragmore whelp wasn't happy about his predicament, in particular being forced to sleep in the same bed as Henry. That plan was actually part of how Henry intended to control the boy and protect himself. He was a light sleeper in the way of all soldiers and would know instantly if Kellen tried to sneak out and grab a sword or a knife. Henry was completely confident in his ability to physically control the lad. He was more than a head taller and nearly twice his weight. And although Kellen was fit, he lacked Henry's musculature. There would be no contest about who would come out victorious if they wrestled. Actually, the thought of getting his hands on that body even in a fight was tempting enough to make his dick rise, not that he would act on the desire. Kellen was his prisoner, after all, and Henry had zero tolerance for sexual violence while on a campaign. He could do no less than he expected of his men.

This winter could prove more difficult than I ever imagined.

Henry rose, suddenly restless and in no more mood to discuss anything. "We shall call it a night, gentlemen. Thank you for your fine counsel, as always."

To a man, they filed out quickly and efficiently, leaving only Colin, who sauntered up to him with his hands behind his back. "Am I to assume I must find somewhere else to sup?"

Henry forced his gaze away from Kellen, where it had wandered on its own, to face his friend. "I'm afraid so. Lord Kellen and I need to get to know one another."

Colin grinned. "Well then, there is a doe-eyed camp follower who has made it very clear he'd welcome my company. I think I'll bring him an offering of a fine meal and see where that takes me."

"As if there's any doubt as to the outcome." Henry clasped his friend on the shoulder. "I'll see you in the morning."

"Unless your charming guest slides a knife between your ribs."

Henry gave a mock shudder. "Don't give him any ideas."

Colin pursed his lips and stared at Kellen before saying, "I don't think he needs me for that. I suspect there's more going on in that pretty head of his than he lets on." With that observation, Colin left.

Frederic passed him coming in, carrying the supper tray, laden with food for two. He put it down on the table and started to set the places, just as he would if Colin or anyone else were dining with Henry. *Clever boy.* He didn't need to be told that the prisoner was to be treated like a guest.

When he was done, Henry waved toward the table. "Come and sit, my lord." When Kellen hesitated, staring at his folded hands in his lap, he added, "I hope you're not planning on refusing out of some misplaced sense of duty to resist."

Lifting his chin, the boy gave him a haughty look. "Certainly not. I'm famished, as it happens. My last meal was at dawn." So saying, he rose with admirable grace and dignity and walked over to the table.

When the boy headed for the seat at the far end, Henry held out the chair next to his own. "Sit here, if you please. I don't want to shout the length of the table to speak with you." He smiled invitingly.

With a sniff, Kellen took the seat. "As you wish, my lord. I guess you're not worried about my sticking a knife in your heart."

Ah, he'd heard after all. "Not in the least," he assured the boy, sitting down, "if for no other reason than Frederic is serving us a hearty stew. We only have spoons."

His squire grinned as he served Henry up first, then Lord Kellen. "It's venison, my lord. There was a successful hunt this afternoon."

"From my father's forest," Kellen muttered as he draped his napkin over his lap.

Henry settled himself in much the same way and reached for the decanter of wine. "Which he's left unguarded while he hides in Highrock." He filled his guest's glass, then his own.

Kellen said nothing at the obvious dig at the duke's treachery. Instead, he picked up his spoon and took a bite of the stew. "Your cook is very good."

Surprised by the normality of the compliment, Henry sipped at his wine before answering. "An army does march on its stomach, and during a siege, it's best to feed soldiers well. Try the wine and tell me what you think." He watched the boy pick up his glass and study it.

Kellen swirled the wine for a few seconds and breathed in its bouquet deeply before drinking some. He tipped his head. "Full-bodied with a hint of currants. A good compliment to the stew." He put the glass down and started in on his meal again.

Henry couldn't help being mesmerized by the sight of the boy devouring his dinner. That he was hungry was obvious, and Henry got some satisfaction in providing for him. More, though, it was a matter of how fascinating it was to watch Kellen's lips wrapping around the spoon, his mouth moving with delicate chewing and his slender neck swallowing it all down. The sight of it all made Henry's groin tighten, and he nearly forgot that he, too, was hungry.

Pausing with his spoon halfway to his mouth, Kellen raised his eyebrows at him. "What?"

Slight flummoxed at being caught staring, Henry shrugged. "Nothing." He shoved a spoonful of venison and potatoes into his mouth and spent the next few minutes concentrating on eating his meal. There was a loaf of fresh bread to bolster the already hearty stew. With his mouth still full, Henry reached for it and tore off a large chunk. He handed it over to Kellen before taking some for himself.

They ate in silence, the only sounds being spoons scraping against bowls and their mutual chewing. Henry continued to have a hard time not focusing his attention on every little move his guest made. It was astounding how something as simple as someone eating was as captivating as an exotic dancer revealing bits of skin throughout a dance.

Kellen finished first and sat back with the glass in his hand, sipping at his wine. His gaze landed on anything other than Henry.

Frederic stepped forward. "Would you like more stew, my lord?"

Kellen seemed surprised the squire was addressing him. "Oh, um, no, thank you. It was delicious, but it doesn't take much to fill me up."

Henry pictured the flat belly he'd spied as the boy had changed earlier. No surprise he was full already. The boy was slender as a reed. He put down his spoon and dabbed his mouth with his napkin. "You'll finish your wine, though?"

Kellen swirled the glass again and stared at the liquid as it dripped down the inner sides. "There's always room for wine." He gulped the remainder, then reached for the decanter.

Henry pulled it out of his reach without thinking. "One glass is enough. Small as you are, you'll be tipsy before we know it." He held the decanter out to Frederic to take it.

Kellen glared at Henry. "I'm not a child."

Henry leaned back to give his squire room to clear the table. "No, you're all grown up—barely. Still, I wouldn't want anyone to think I got you drunk to take advantage of you." He grinned.

"Impossible. I never drink to excess, and not even alcohol would make me impressed with your charms, my lord."

Henry winced. "My pride is wounded, but I was referring to my trying to wheedle useful information out of you. Nothing more personal than that, although..."

Kellen crossed his arms. "You'll get nothing out of me on either account. However I might feel about my father's scheme to create his own kingdom, I will never betray him. And I don't lie with men."

Henry clasped his chest over his heart. "I am wounded to hear it." Pushing aside the fact that he was actually disappointed at the boy's vehement dismissal, he picked at his guest still in the hopes of drawing out more information that might prove useful. "So, there is a girl within the castle waiting for you?"

Kellen rolled his eyes. "I didn't say that. I'm too busy to be entangled with anyone."

The relief that rushed through Henry was disconcerting. "Ah yes, your winemaking. An interesting choice of vocation for a duke's son."

"As the youngest, I didn't have many choices. My brother was the heir, and with his passing, it's my sister. I have no aptitude for governing, and I'm not suited to soldiering."

Henry rested his chin on his palm, not even bothering to hide his fascination with his guest. "You are quite small."

Kellen slumped in his chair. "That's really not the issue. Isolde is not much bigger than I am, but she has the disposition of a warrior and is an excellent archer." He turned to stare at Henry. "You don't want to get too close to the ramparts. Her bowmen are known for their accuracy."

"Yes, I am aware," Henry drawled. "Believe me when I say that I want this siege to end with as little loss of life on both sides as possible. Thus, I'm prepared to sit here all winter."

"I'm not sure I do believe you. I can't imagine King Auden has given you orders to spare anyone at Highrock."

"That's where you're wrong, my lord." Frederic caught his eye by returning with a small plate covered with a cloth. "What's this?"

"Your pardon, my lord. Cook thought Lord Kellen might appreciate a treat." Putting the plate down, he whipped off the cloth. There sat a pile of four cookies.

Kellen's eyes lit up, and he started to sit forward before catching himself and leaning back again.

The fact that the boy thought he had to hide his excitement at such a small thing made Henry's heart pang with pity. He wondered if Kellen's reticence came from the no doubt frightening situation of being a prisoner of the man sent to defeat his father or whether this was behavior learned in childhood. No matter... Henry was determined to be as kind to the boy as he could be.

Not one for sweets, he nevertheless picked up two cookies from the plate. He held out one to Kellen. "I trust you have a little bit more room in your stomach for dessert."

The boy eyed him with obvious distrust before taking the offering. The look on his face when he bit into the cookie reminded Henry disconcertingly of how someone looked when orgasming.

"Hmm. This is very tasty." He gave Henry a sideways glance. "I don't suppose you have any port?"

Henry gestured toward Frederic while keeping his gaze on Kellen. When his squire poured two small glasses of the sweet, heavy wine, Henry ate bites of his cookie between sips without taking his eyes off his guest. It was captivating to watch Kellen enjoy both the treat and the drink. The sight did funny things to his belly, and his cock and balls ached with their confinement. He wondered how he'd manage an entire winter entertaining this boy if the first night was driving him crazy. It was hard not to tug at his trousers to give his genitals more room.

When Kellen had polished off two cookies and his port, he sat back and looked pointedly at Henry. "What now, my lord?"

Henry's mind scrambled with sudden visions of how to answer that. He mentally shook his head. "Hmm? Oh, how about a game of chess? You do play, don't you?" Most nobles preferred card games, he knew, but chess was a close second as a post-dinner pastime. *And it's boringly safe.*

"Yes. I'm quite good, actually."

"Excellent. I like a challenge." He waved at Frederic and waited until the squire had positioned the board on the table for them before saying. "You may go now. I won't need you anymore."

Frederic sketched a bow. "Yes, my lord. I'll see you in the morning."

A look of panic crossed Kellen's face. "He's leaving?"

Henry leaned on elbow on the table. "Yes. I don't need someone to undress me. Frederic deserves time to himself as much as the next man, too." He couldn't help grinning. "Why? Are you worried about being alone with me?"

Kellen sniffed and pulled his chair closer to the table. "Certainly not. I don't need a knife to defend myself, either."

"Your virtue is safe with me, Lord Kellen. Never fear." Even as he said the words, he wasn't entirely sure they were true. Sleeping beside this boy and not touching him was going to tax his self-control and his honor. He put thoughts of the night aside before his head and other things exploded. "Black or white?"

"I don't care."

"Confident, aren't we? The white pieces are in front of you, so let's go with that."

"Very well." Kellen didn't hesitate to move his first pawn.

No slouch in the game himself, Henry made his move quickly as well. Kellen countered with obvious confidence. It didn't take long for him to see the pattern that was emerging, and the boy was going to be a worthy opponent. Colin was a decent enough player, but Kellen was good — very good. Soon, Henry was so absorbed in the game that he forgot he'd intended to try to pump information out of the duke's son. Pieces came off the board with alacrity, and the pile was growing faster on Kellen's side of the table.

As Henry pondered his latest move, the boy picked up the last cookie and took a big bite. "Don't tax yourself, my lord. I'm going to checkmate you in three moves, no matter what you do."

Annoyed, Henry frowned at him. "The devil you are!" He hovered his fingers over the pieces in unusual hesitation before making his next more.

Kellen popped the last of his cookie into his mouth before countering. "I was wrong. It's only going to take me two. One now." The boy's expression was one of defiance, but there was a wariness in his eyes, as if expecting news of his victory was going to result in trouble.

Ignoring the spurt of sympathy he felt, Henry studied the board before knocking his king on its side with a sigh. "Damnation." Resting his chin once more on his palm, he stared at the boy. "You are an excellent player. No one has given me that kind of competition in a very long while."

Kellen tossed his head, and now there was relief in his underlying expression. "People underestimate me."

And expect you to lose to avoid their wrath. He felt a kind of pride that the boy wasn't cowed into losing deliberately, not that he had any right or reason for feeling that way. "I'll endeavor not to do so."

The boy let out a loud yawn, blinking at him owlishly. "Sorry. The nuns get up with the sun. I guess I'm tired." With a start, he sat up straighter. "Not that I need to go to sleep. How about another game?"

Henry nearly smiled, but the boy's apprehension, if not fear, was obvious. He needed to be kind, even if it killed him. Pushing back his chair, he stood. "No. It's time for bed — for both of us. I get up at dawn myself." He waved toward the bed. "Come on."

Kellen stood with obvious reluctance. "I'm not sleeping in that bed with you. I'll lie down in that corner over there."

"Absolutely not. I don't intend to restrain you so long as you sleep in my bed, because as a soldier, I wake easily and instantly. With you lying beside me, I'll know if you try to get up. If you are elsewhere, I might not rouse, and that would be troublesome for both of us."

Kellen's chest rose and fell on a deep breath. "Surely there are guards all around this tent. I can't escape."

"That's true, but I won't jeopardize any of my men with my decision to keep you unconfined." He sighed. "I promise I won't touch you. I'm no rapist, my lord."

"And I'm not as delicate as you might perceive. Try something and you'll see I'm more of my father's son than you think."

There was pride and determination in those words and something else—vulnerability. *He's scared.* It wasn't a big revelation, more obvious than anything else. Being a nobleman, the boy hid his feelings better than most, but he was young and in the clutches of his enemy, at least to his way of thinking. Henry needed to keep that in mind. As much as he hoped something useful could be had from this unexpected turn of events, he also had a duty to protect his prisoner, from himself as much as from anyone else.

Henry started going around the tent to turn down the lamps. "Prepare yourself for bed, my lord. Pick whichever side you prefer, and I shall stick to the far end of the other." He was used to lying dead center unless he had a companion for the night, and even then, he normally would stick close to his bed partner for pleasure. This was going to be different. He would have to learn to keep his hands — and everything else — to himself.

Kellen hesitated a few moments more before sitting on the bed to pull off his boots. Henry paid him no mind until he saw the boy intended to get under the covers fully clothed.

"What are you doing?"

Kellen peered over at him with wary eyes. "Getting into bed."

"You must undress first."

The boy's expression went from alarmed to irritated. "Why?"

"Because you'll need them as fresh as possible for the daytime. I don't know where Frederic managed to find them, but I doubt it's an endless well of bounty. You can keep your smallclothes on if you wish."

"Thank you for your magnanimity, my lord baron." The biting tone was diminished somewhat by the blush on the boy's cheeks. The color was barely visible in the light of the one remaining lamp…and it was adorable.

To give the boy privacy and to keep his own body in check, Henry poked at the brazier to bank for the fire for the night. By the time he returned to the bed, his guest was buried under the covers, gazing at the top of the tent. The boy was as far over to the edge as he could get without tumbling out.

Henry turned down the last lamp to make it as dark as he could before stripping himself. He never wore smallclothes, not seeing a need for the extra layer to deal with, but he wished he did at that moment. Of course he remained hard as he'd been since first setting eyes on the duke's fetching son. His cock sprang from its confines without hesitation, and not wanting to alarm Kellen, Henry kept his back to him and slid into bed on his side facing away from him. He was damned uncomfortable, but there was no hope for it. The last thing he intended to do was to take his dick in hand and give himself release. He could think of little else that would be more provocative in the boy's eyes.

"Sleep well, Lord Kellen." He meant what he said, too. One of them might as well, and for damn sure, he wasn't going to.

Chapter Three

Kellen woke surprised that he'd slept at all. When he'd first slipped into bed, he'd been so anxious that he'd expected to lie all night awake and watchful. No matter Roth's promises, Kellen had no illusions about how powerful men, particularly those who were soldiers, thought everything in the world was theirs to take. He'd spent the last few years avoiding the greedy stares and grasping hands of his father's men and guests. He knew how much they coveted him and was just as sure that he wouldn't like anything they had planned. But his captor had stayed true to his word and had stuck to his side of the bed. It had been particularly surprising, given how Kellen had glimpsed the man's state of arousal. Even in the gloom, the man's large, hard cock had flashed a warning before being covered up. Kellen had laid there for the gods knew how long waiting for the man to roll over and make a grab for him. When instead, the baron's breathing had evened out with sleep, Kellen had been relieved and oddly a little disappointed.

Don't be ridiculous.

His captor was at the far side of the tent, breaking his fast and deep in discussion with that tall man he called Colin. Their ease with each other spoke of a long-time friendship that transcended their disparate positions. And as with before, he sensed there was an intimacy between the two men. Once again, he admonished himself to stop dwelling on that fact. It was of no consequence to him.

Frederic arrived and broke his line of sight. The squire held a bowl and a small towel. "Good morning, my lord. I've come to help you with your morning ablutions and getting dressed." The boy put the items down on a low table and pulled a chamber pot out from under it. "Would you like to use this first?"

Kellen did need to, actually, given that he hadn't had a chance to relieve himself since he'd changed out of his nun's habit. It seemed a lifetime ago since his capture. He rose, one eye on the baron, and turned his back to give himself some measure of privacy. Frederic was good at his job, busying himself with snapping Kellen's tunic to unfold it and lay it on the bed. When Kellen was done, the squire helped him wash and dress, although Kellen demurred over the boy's efforts to tug his boots on.

"I can do that. Thank you."

The squire grabbed the chamber pot, bowl and towel before bowing. "My pleasure, Lord Kellen. Breakfast is laid out on the table. The baron won't mind your helping yourself."

Kellen paused in the middle of tugging on his second boot. "He looks busy."

Frederic chuckled. "He's always that, my lord."

Rumblings from his empty stomach prodded him to stand and go over to the table. He eyed the two men as he did so, waiting for any kind of rebuke. None came. Instead, Roth broke off from what he was saying long enough to gesture for Kellen to take a seat and serve himself breakfast. Kellen did so, but he knew better than to let down his guard. He kept one eye on the men as he filled his plate with eggs, buttered toast and honey to drizzle over it.

Colin spoke before the baron continued. "I wish you'd reconsider your plan to go into town, my lord."

Roth didn't answer right away. He pushed a pot sitting on a trivet in Kellen's direction. "Have some tea."

Being thirsty and careful to pick his battles, Kellen filled a nearby cup and doctored it with some of the honey. It was strong and warm and helped his food slide down more easily. He wanted to close his eyes to savor the pleasure of such fine food after days of having the nuns' bland provisions, yet he didn't want to give Roth the satisfaction that he was enjoying any part of his captivity.

A slight smile graced the man's lips, as if he knew what Kellen was thinking and feeling before he turned his attention back to his man. "I hear your concerns, Colin, and appreciate the wisdom of your advice."

"But you won't take it."

"No. If we're to spend the winter here, it's important that the townspeople see that our soldiers are under the command of someone who trusts them enough to walk among them. I want to reassure the guild masters that we are here to buy their wares, not confiscate them. Everyone's safety depends on our having a good relationship with these folks. The duke's men can't get to us anymore than we can get to them. We must guard our flanks and rear from aggression from those outside the castle walls."

Kellen didn't even try to hide the fact that he was listening, his gaze fixed on the men even as he shoveled food into his mouth. One of his biggest fears was the king's men would grow bored and frustrated with the siege and amuse themselves by sacking the town and the surrounding farmlands. He'd studied enough history to know that it was a real possibility. The powerful rarely contained their disputes to themselves. Ordinary people always suffered when there was warfare. If Roth was to be believed, the man was sufficiently decent to make sure the soldiers under his command behaved themselves — or maybe he was just worried that any aggression on their part would inspire the local population to attack them in turn. No matter, it was the result that was important, regardless of the motivation.

The baron turned his attention back to Kellen. "Are you enjoying your breakfast, my lord?"

Kellen shrugged. "I think I was clear last night that your cook is very good. My complaints don't lie with the food."

Roth laughed. "I trust you have none about my conduct last night. I was true to my word, was I not?"

Kellen grimaced, hating the change in topic. He didn't like the reminder that they'd shared a bed, and he really didn't like the smirk on Sir Colin's face. "Showing restraint in that way is a very low standard to hold yourself to, my lord." He bit off a chunk of toast while glaring at his captor.

Far from being insulted, the infuriating man merely laughed again. "I can't argue with that point." He turned to Colin. "You know, Lord Kellen is an excellent chess player. Very good at strategy. Better than you, certainly."

Sir Colin shrugged. "That's not hard to be. It's not my game. I only play it to amuse you and make you feel good about winning."

Kellen froze, astounded at the man's audacity.

The baron merely laughed yet again. "Well, Lord Kellen felt no such compunction. He trounced me handily. Didn't you, my lord?" When Kellen merely rolled his eyes, the man dropped the subject. "Finish up quickly now. You'll be coming with me."

Kellen swallowed his mouthful. "For what reason? I don't need to be in your constant sight. You can't possibly think I'll somehow sneak out of this tent and make my way through your camp with no one noticing?"

Roth reached over and snagged the last piece of toast. "Certainly not. Perhaps I simply enjoy your company." He stood as he took a bite. "Frederic!"

The squire came running in, obviously waiting outside to be summoned. "Yes, my lord?"

"Fetch my cloak and one for Lord Kellen." He stuffed the rest of the toast in his mouth. "It's a chilly morning."

Frederic gnawed at his lower lip. "I'm sorry, my lord. I'm not sure where I can find one the right size that isn't already being used by its owner."

"Hmm, well give him one of mine then. He'll swim in it, but it will have to do until I can buy one for him in town."

In quick order, Kellen was up and wrapped in a simple wool cloak with a fur collar that made him look like a little boy trying on his father's clothing, not that he'd ever done such a thing. He had to gather them up in his arms to keep from tripping. He felt like a lady holding her skirts to keep them out of the mud, but the moment he left the tent, he appreciated the warmth.

The temperature had dropped significantly from the day before. Having lived in the North his entire life, he knew how quickly winter would descend. Already he sensed snow was coming.

As he trudged through the camp, he made a point of keeping his head up. All the soldiers and other people milling about the camp stared openly at him. He was a curiosity that broke up the tedium of their day, no doubt. He wasn't going to give anyone the satisfaction of thinking he was cowed. Being the son of a duke had given him a measure of pride, despite how low in authority he was in Highrock. He took note, as well, of the layout of the sprawling community that had taken up residence in the large field surrounding the castle. The king's men were well-provisioned, having sufficient weaponry to win once the confrontation began—and it would. Highrock had a large store of provisions, but they would run out sometime around the spring thaw, or perhaps last through most of summer if they rationed very carefully. If his father had thought the king would lose interest in him, he was wrong. These soldiers were there for as long as it took, and they could re-provision themselves endlessly. He could only hope that his father would come to his senses before too many people within the castle suffered from starvation.

As they weaved through the crowd, Roth's men greeted him with affable respect. More, they appeared to genuinely like him. That was something unexpected. None of his father's men liked him overly much, as near as he could tell. It had been the same with his brother. Wilfred had had a few close friends, bound mostly by their mutual joy in tormenting others, but Kellen had seen the looks of hatred in other men's eyes when Wilfred hadn't been looking. No one showed much grief, however, at his passing, that was for certain. And Isolde intimidated everyone with her capricious temper. The castle denizens gave her a wide berth. So Roth's popularity among his men was novel for Kellen, and he couldn't help admiring the man for it.

As they approached the edge of the town, a contingent of a half-dozen soldiers joined them, two on each side and in the back. It wasn't a big show of force, just enough to keep Roth safe while also communicating that he wasn't afraid to walk among the townsfolk. Of course, their arrival caused everything to come to a halt as everyone stopped what they were doing to stare at them. He knew some of these people, and the looks of concern they sent his way warmed him. He tried to convey with his own expression that there was no need to worry on his account. It occurred to him suddenly that this was maybe the real reason for the baron bringing him along—to ensure that word spread if it hadn't already that the baron had Kellen. He probably thought it would reach the castle in some fashion. But if the man thought the duke would be moved by his son's plight to surrender, he was going to be disappointed. It hadn't been bravado when he'd warned his captor that his father probably hadn't noticed that he was no longer in the castle or cared either way.

At the center of the town stood the guild house, and in front of it was gathered all of the guild masters and mistresses. Obviously, the baron had sent word that he wanted to speak with them. They all watched the man's approach with a mixture of concern and anger. Nothing was outwardly hostile, of course, but they weren't good at hiding their thoughts and emotions. If Kellen could see it, so could the baron. He feared what the man might do if he was insulted.

Roth stopped in front of the group and inclined his head. "Good morning. Thank you for answering my invitation."

The mistress of the weavers sniffed. "Oh, did we have a choice, my lord? It seemed to be more of a summons, coming as it did by the hand of a group of your soldiers." There was a noticeable increase in the tension in the air.

Roth merely smiled. "I stand corrected, madam. I didn't expect any of you to refuse, but this meeting is to our mutual benefit, I assure you." He held his hand up, and Sir Colin placed a rolled-up parchment in it. "I had my quartermaster create a list of provisions we expect to need throughout the coming winter. I think you'll find the prices we propose to pay more than fair." He held the document out to the mistress of the weavers.

The woman couldn't hide her surprise as she took and unfurled it. All the guild leaders crowded around her to get a look at what the king's man was demanding. There were some nods and murmurs, then the paper was passed around so that each person could study it more closely. Finally, the master of the poulters stepped forward with it in hand.

"Seems fair enough, my lord." He handed it back.

Roth smiled. "Excellent." He sent it back to Colin. "My quartermaster will be in touch with each of you in kind as our needs arise. Again, I thank you for coming, and please go about your day."

The poulter stopped him before he turned away. "Wait, my lord. What about the boy?"

Roth raised his eyebrows, seeming more amused than annoyed. "What about him?" He didn't bother to pretend he didn't understand who the man was referring to.

"Lord Kellen is a good lad. Anyone will tell you that." He cleared his throat. "We don't like that he's your prisoner."

Kellen blinked at the man a few times, surprised and touched to learn that anyone in town paid him any mind, let alone thought well of him. He didn't want to repay such kindness by allowing them to stick out their necks on his behalf. "I am well, Master Poulter. Please do not concern yourself on my behalf."

The townspeople didn't seem convinced, but Roth gave them no chance to respond.

"See? He still has his tongue." He grabbed one of Kellen's hands and held it up. "His fingernails are intact, as is the rest of him. You have my word he will not be harmed. I trust that is the end of it." Now the man's tone implied that he wasn't going to indulge the townspeople in any further challenge to his authority.

The master poulter grimaced. "As you say, my lord."

"Good, now I wonder if you might point me in the direction of a shop where I may purchase a cloak?"

When the directions were given, the baron inclined his head once more and left. He kept his hold on Kellen's hand, and when he tried to free it, the man tightened his grip. It was ridiculous to be led about like a child, but also…intriguing how the baron's touch warmed Kellen more than the cloak did.

The haberdashers was close by, and the man who owned it came out to greet the baron with wringing hands. "How may I help you, my lord?"

"I am in need of a cloak." As he said it, he wandered over to pegs where many hung.

"Of course, my lord, but I fear you might need a tailor to custom-make one. You are, um, very tall and, ah, broad, if I may say so. We don't usually stock anything that big."

Roth looked at the man from over his shoulder. "Not for me. For him." He nodded in Kellen's direction.

"Oh, of course. Forgive my gaffe, my lord. These over here are made for older children and would likely fit Lord Kellen very well."

Kellen ignored the spurt of irritation at being compared to a child. He was small. There was no denying that. Roth tugged him to the display and let his hand go in order to pick through the options himself. Perversely, Kellen missed the contact the moment it was broken.

The baron held up a light blue cloak with silver thread embroidered through it and a dark fur collar. It was lined with the same fur. "This looks about right." He gestured to Colin, who had stuck to their sides, even as the other soldiers stood farther back. "Take that one off."

Before Kellen could object, the knight whipped the oversized cloak off his body and Roth replaced it with the one he was holding. Then the man fussed with it, making sure it draped properly on Kellen's shoulders and closing the clasp at the neck.

"Yes, excellent." Roth's lips twitched up. "And it brings out the color in your eyes."

Irritated at the comment, Kellen put his hands on his hips. "I don't need anything this grand. A simple wool one will do nicely."

"Nonsense. You are the son of a duke, and as you are my responsibility, I will see that you are afforded all of the courtesies your station demands. Pay the man, Colin," he added before taking Kellen by the elbow and whisking him away.

Kellen tugged himself free. "Your largesse and attention embarrass me."

"Does it? Dear me, you're going to have to get used to it, I'm afraid...unless you have a way to break this siege."

Kellen's heart skipped a beat. Here was the thing he feared most about being Roth's prisoner—that he would extract information out of him. *I must be strong.* "I can be of no help to you, my lord."

Roth signed. "That was what I thought. No matter... Let's go have a ride. My horse needs the exercise."

Kellen tripped over his own feet with surprise. "A ride?"

"Yes, you do know how to sit a horse, do you not?"

"Of course, but..." He wasn't sure what to say. It seemed inconceivable that the man would dare to give him such freedom. Then again, he was never going to try to escape. That wouldn't end well. He was sure of it. Perhaps this ride was a ploy to get him to try in order for him to lead them to a way into the castle. That was never going to happen, and the baron wasn't stupid enough to believe it, was he? *No. Someone as good at chess as he was wouldn't be so foolish.* Because it was impossible for him to second-guess the man, he gave up trying. "That would be nice, actually."

* * * *

Henry found himself more excited than he would have expected at the prospect of spending the day with his prisoner. It was true that he had the ulterior motive of catching the boy's reaction to the place he intended to take him to see if some amount of useful information could be gleaned. It was also true, however, that riding beside him, watching that beautiful blond hair whipping around the equally beautiful face was a delight. Just looking at Kellen made Henry's heartbeat quicken, and his cock was in a permanent semi-hard state. Being cramped inside his trousers was uncomfortable for sure, but in an oddly pleasurable way. It was the anticipation of possibly finding release at some point that increased his pleasure. Since the age of sixteen, he'd become accustomed to knowing release was within easy reach. The fact that seducing Kellen was both a thing to avoid for the sake of honor and that the boy would resist no matter what made the arousal that much greater.

How utterly perverse I am.

As he cantered toward the cliffs of Highrock, the small mare that the horse master had given Kellen lagged only a little with Henry' bigger warhorse, and he decided he didn't care. It was a glorious day, despite the chill. His personal guard kept back a good distance as he'd ordered. Henry felt safe enough and could handle himself, regardless. Kellen's obvious and excellent seat gave Henry the confidence that the boy could handle the fast pace. And while there was a reason Henry had chosen this direction, it didn't change the fact that he loved watching the roiling sea as they approached. He'd been raised far inland but had loved the ocean from the first time he'd seen it. If nothing else, an outing along the beach would be enjoyable for its own sake.

He reined up before they reached the cliffside. Kellen brought his horse alongside Henry's, his pale cheeks flushed from the windy ride. The boy's gaze shifted to the left, where his father's castle stood, but only for a second before he fixed it at the shoreline below them.

"Do you like riding along the sand?" Henry kept his tone casual, even though he knew the duke's son was too clever not to understand why they were there.

Without looking at him, Kellen answered. "Anyone raised by the sea does." Then he glanced in Henry's direction. "There is a path down to it over there that the horses can navigate, although I expect you know that already."

Henry couldn't help chuckling. "My men have been very thorough in their explorations, so yes, I do. Come." He wheeled his horse to the right and made his way over to the natural sandy pathway down the cliff to the beach.

Being a warhorse, his mount was rock steady, placing his hooves correctly to navigate the steep path with ease. One glance back assured him that Kellen had his horse well in hand. The mare was more careful in her steps but soon reached the flat sand to stand once more beside Henry's. Both horses tossed their heads, noses up, taking in the bracing sea air as much as their riders. There was something uniquely enjoyable about the salty wind and the sound of gulls screeching overhead. It was peaceful in a counterintuitive sort of way. Henry gave himself a few seconds to enjoy his surroundings before taking up his duties.

He led Kellen slowly to the hard, wet sand being exposed by the retreating tide. Once they were on surer footing, he kicked his horse into a canter, then a full-on gallop. Kellen followed without being told, keeping pace in an impressive way. The horses' hooves splashed through the foamy edge of the water. The wind whipped hair and manes alike behind them as they headed toward the cliff where Highrock stood — dark and bleak and soaring toward the sky. It looked foreboding and impregnable on this side, and as they approached the cliffside beneath it, the stone was jagged and unbroken.

The Cragmore family had chosen well where to build the seat of their power. As his men had reported, no break in the rock could be seen, and any man trying to climb it was doomed to fall at some point. There simply wasn't anywhere to gain hand or toe holds all the way up, and even if one were to accomplish that climb, Highrock's wall was solid with no entry points at all. Plus, archers stationed on the ramparts would have no trouble picking them off.

Henry slowed his horse down, then stopped it far enough away so that if there were any such archers on the ramparts facing in that direction, their arrows would fall short. He took in and let out a long breath. "Such a beautiful spot—and clearly not a way into the castle." He turned to look at Kellen to see if the boy's expression gave anything away.

It didn't.

Kellen returned his gaze with a bland look, seemingly effortlessly controlling his horse that was frisky from the brisk ride. "That's why my ancestor chose to build here. Three sides are easier to defend than four." He turned away again. "If you came here looking for useful information to end the siege in your favor, you've wasted your time."

Henry didn't bother to hide his amusement. He chuckled before saying, "I beg to differ. Information is always useful, but an invigorating ride through the surf with an exquisite companion by my side is reason enough to come here." He nearly bit his tongue at its indiscretion, but the words had popped out before he could stop them.

Kellen tossed his head much as his horse was doing. "Your blandishments are wasted on me, Baron. I don't care what you think of me." He turned his face away again, although his cheeks appeared to redden even more than they had from the wind.

"You know, Lord Kellen, I don't think I believe you." It was an intemperate thing to say, but once again, he couldn't help himself. "I bet no one has ever paid you the right kind of attention, showing respect as well as interest. You're used to steering clear of men for the sake of your safety, are you not?" Henry didn't know why he pressed the matter. There was something about this boy that made him want to protect and soothe. He sensed a lifetime of hurt in Kellen, and healing it suddenly became important to him.

The set of Kellen's expression told him he'd hit a nerve, yet the boy raised his chin and said, "You know nothing about me or my life and...I don't need your pity, if that's what this is. You are my enemy and are only trying to exploit a perceived weakness."

Henry felt a deep pang of that very emotion Kellen was trying to throw in his face. Still, Kellen was entitled to his pride, and Henry didn't want to cause him more hurt than he was already. "You're not my enemy, Kellen. I'm only here to bring your father to heel for the sake of our country. I won't hurt you," he added in a low voice.

There was a flash of some unnamable emotion in the boy's eyes as he whipped his head in Henry' direction. "Men like you have a very narrow definition of what hurting means. You have no idea what harm can be done to people held prisoner to your power. You'll always twist your actions in your own mind to convince yourself you're right in what you are doing. It doesn't matter anyway," he added, looking away once more.

Henry opened his mouth, wanting to argue the point. He was sure he understood the nuance of what Kellen was saying. He was a self-aware man and understood that words could cut as deeply as steel. He was rather feeling the effect of that very thing at the moment. Kellen's dismissal of him was poking a hole in him that he wouldn't have thought he was vulnerable to.

There was no point in discussing anything further. He'd gotten what he'd wanted out of the ride — both exercise and knowledge. If Kellen knew of a weakness in the rock cliff, he hid it well. It was also time for the midday meal, and he was famished.

Turning his horse around, he said, "It's time to go back to camp." He took off, certain the boy would follow and wishing it were because he wanted to and not in fear of the consequences if he didn't.

Chapter Four

It was Henry's habit to eat with his men during luncheon. He spent so much time in his tent, conferring with his advisors and taking his breakfast and dinner there, that midday was the perfect time for him to show his face and connect with the average soldier. He knew plenty of troop leaders who kept their distance. They thought it added to their superiority and the respect their men needed to show them. They weren't merely one of the many soldiers. They were high above them. Henry felt quite differently. He *was* one of fighting men, bloodied as they all were through battle. When the time came to charge any enemy, he would lead from the front and not behind, safe from the risk of war.

He kept Kellen by his side as he wandered through the camp toward the huge open kitchen area set up to feed the troops. It wasn't necessary to bring the boy with him. Frederic could have brought food to him in Henry's tent, and as Kellen had pointed out many times, he'd be well-guarded, even without Henry being there. Still, he couldn't quite hand the boy over. There was a driving need to have Cragmore's son remain with him. And the way the boy stuck close to his side — undoubtedly out of fear of the soldiers than any desire — was gratifying. It didn't take more than a narrow-eyed glance at all of his men who showed too much interest to ward off any predation. Kellen was safe with him.

Henry greeted each of the soldiers he passed, as was his habit. He knew many of them by name as well as by face. If the siege lasted all winter, he would learn each soldier's name. His memory was phenomenal, and the personal touch mattered to him. He cared about his men and knew that they, in turn, appreciated that he took the time to know them more personally. They weren't merely indistinguishable sacrifices to the king's glory. Their pain was his, and he never sent soldiers to their possible deaths without knowing he would mourn every loss of life.

The head cook was actually a woman whose career as a soldier had been cut short by an injury that had left her with a limp. And yes, some of his men were actually women. He appreciated them even more because he knew no one had expected or encouraged them to pick soldiering as their path in life. To have chosen and worked for it anyway made those women to be among his most dedicated soldiers.

Madge was now a middle-aged woman, but she had the strength and vigor of a more youthful person. Her younger helpers had to hustle to keep up with her. She greeted him with a broad smile that showed how many of her teeth had been lost to fighting.

"My lord, you are right on time, as usual. Have a seat and let's see if my humble efforts please you — and your guest, of course," she added with a not unkindly pointed look at Kellen.

Even knowing there was no menace there, Henry put his arm around the boy's shoulder. Not surprisingly, Kellen stiffened at the touch. "You have an admirer already, Mistress Madge, in Lord Kellen. He was particularly fond of your cookies."

Madge put her hands on her hips. "Naturally. A well-bred lad knows good food when he tastes it. Here...sit." She waved at the seat where Henry usually took his meals. It was among the many places set to accommodate those who ate, although it was nothing more than stout logs.

He led Kellen over and removed his arm as the boy sat down. He felt the lack of touch immediately and made up for it by sitting close enough to Kellen that their hips touched.

Once more, Kellen stiffened. "Might I have more *space*, Baron?"

Henry held back the grin threatening to erupt. It wouldn't do for him to tease the young lord in front of the men. "I'm sorry, but this log has to accommodate as many as possible." That was true, although naturally, he could take up as much room as he wanted. He wasn't going to admit that he liked touching the boy no matter what, though.

The log in which they sat did fill up with others, his soldiers not being shy about joining him. The other logs around them did as well. This scene was being played out all around the campsite. The soldiers ate in shifts, of course, rotating their duties to keep watch. There were still dozens being fed at any one time. And while he was greeted as usual, everyone around them studiously ignored Kellen. Word had gotten around that the baron's guest was not to be trifled with, even by a casual look. After a while, Kellen visibly relaxed.

While the other men had obtained their food and drink by standing in the chow line, one of the cook's helpers brought Henry and Kellen their meals. It was simple, yet hearty, thick sandwiches filled with meat and cheese. Each was also given a tankard of cider. Kellen thanked the serving boy, balanced his plate on his lap and placed his drink on the ground beside him. He bit into his sandwich with obvious hunger. Henry permitted himself a few seconds of enjoyment watching the boy eat before doing the same.

"A brisk ride and the sea air works up an appetite, does it not?" Henry asked between mouthfuls.

"Hmm," was Kellen's only reply. He kept his gaze on his meal and didn't bother to look at Henry.

That irked for some reason. *I'm acting like a schoolboy with his first crush.* Determined not to be lured by Kellen's appeal, Henry turned his attention to the soldiers around them. He asked about how their day was going.

He sensed some reluctance by the men to talk much openly around what was effectively the enemy, but eventually followed Henry's example as he continued to discuss their activities in detail. He really wasn't worried about what Kellen heard or learned about them. It would be impossible for the duke to mount a rescue, even if he decided his son was worth the risk — which he sadly doubted very much. And perhaps it was naïve of him, but something told him that even if Kellen was before his father and held strategic information, the boy wouldn't give it to him. From all that Henry had gleaned, the young lord wasn't happy about his father's efforts to secede from Moorcondia.

He seemed to have rightly assessed that it was a plan that was doomed to failure. Anyone with sense would understand that. It was puzzling that the duke didn't seem to have any.

When the meal was finished, Henry made a point of thanking the cook as he always did. The woman surprised him by handing him something wrapped in cloth.

The woman grinned at his raised eyebrows. "More cookies for the young lord. Boys his age get hungry between meals, do they not?"

Henry took the package yet said nothing. It was a little disconcerting how much her words emphasized in his mind how young Kellen was. *He's little more than a child, not for playing with.* Yes, his intellect was spot on. Too bad his dick was of a different opinion.

"Thank you, mistress, for your kindness," Kellen said, once again proving that he was a polite and kind young man.

Henry returned to his tent, Kellen in his wake, and handed both the cookies and a nearby book to the boy. "Here… This might not be to your liking, but I dare say it will pass the time."

Taking both offerings, Kellen studied the title on the cover of the leather-bound book etched in gold lettering. "I like history, as it happens." He looked Henry in the eye for the first time in what seemed like hours. "It's nice to know that I won't be bored during my imprisonment."

Henry bristled at the description, even though it was apt. "You will be afforded every amenity your station demands. Make yourself comfortable on the bed or in a chair. I must consult with my advisors now and will be gone much of the afternoon."

Kellen gave him what could only be described as a coy look. "You mean I'm to be trusted to be alone in here? You'd better lock up your sharps."

Henry narrowed his gaze and leaned into Kellen's space to reply, perversely happy when the boy's eyes went wide with concern. "Take whatever you like, my lord. I'll be pleased to search you myself upon my return."

Satisfied that he'd made his point, Henry headed for the tent's opening. He stopped and looked over his shoulder, guilt setting in almost immediately. "If you need anything, you only have to poke your head out and ask any of the guards for Frederic. My squire will take care of you."

He left before Kellen could reply, not that he probably cared to. The lack of a comeback also bothered him, because when it came to this boy, apparently rational thought was leaking steadily out of his head.

* * * *

Kellen tossed the book on the low table sitting beside his chair. Being a fast reader, he'd finished it already, and with his stomach filled with cookies, he felt sluggish and sleepy. He eyed the bed, then shook his head. The last thing he needed was for the baron to find him curled up and vulnerable. The man had the upper hand on him already, and there was no point in making himself an easier target.

He stood, stretched and yawned. Looking around, he saw that there was a lot for him to snoop into. It was tempting, but the baron's threat of searching his body upon the man's return was a threat that made fear override his curiosity. He wasn't really going to take a weapon and try to attack his captor anyway. It would be suicide, and no matter how miserable his life had been, Kellen still had a strong will to live.

I can handle whatever he does to me.

His vow would have been more impressive if the baron had done anything untoward. Thus far, there had been no assault and no torture. The worst the man had done was put his arm around his shoulders and press his hip and leg against his own. Those touches were hardly painful, but they were disturbing. He should fear the baron and despise him. Somehow that wasn't happening. Instead, he felt safe with the man, and with the growing amount of time he was spending in the baron's company, a disconcerting part of him was becoming more intrigued by him as a man. The king's commander had been impossibly handsome and impressive as he had galloped his large mount through the surf. His power and confidence were palpable things. Kellen couldn't help but be both impressed and aroused. The mere thought of the time they'd spent together that morning made him need to rearrange his trousers.

He's using me.

Yes, that was all too true. The baron hadn't brought Kellen to the beach simply to have fun. He'd been testing him, seeing if being by the cliffside would cause him to give away any secret he might possess. It hadn't worked. From a very young age, Kellen had mastered how to hide his thoughts and feelings from others. He'd erected those walls without conscious thought and had given nothing of what he knew away. He could only hope that would be the end of it. His biggest fear had become being too complacent in the baron's company and letting his desire for the man override his loyalty to his father. The duke was not a kind man and barely acknowledged his existence. His effort to create his own kingdom was insane on the face of it and had the imprint of Isolde's boldness and rash ambition. That being said, they were still his family, and he wasn't going to betray them. This siege could only end one way, and Kellen didn't want to be the reason why Roth gained access to the castle. The king's man would have every right to slaughter anyone inside. Kellen couldn't live with that blood on his hands.

Henry wouldn't do that.

He blinked hard at his own thoughts. Baron Roth was a stranger to him. He wouldn't have been given this duty by the king if he weren't a consummate soldier—and that meant being a ruthless one as well. That was the way of the world. And yet, as little as he knew about the baron, he had a hard time imagining the man, who made fair trade with the townspeople and bothered to speak with his men no matter how low they were, killing those who merely followed the duke's orders. While there were some mean and ambitious men who did what the duke wanted with relish, most of the people trapped inside the castle were prisoners as much as Kellen was.

Kellen paced around the tent, trying to quiet his thoughts, before putting Roth's words to the test out of uncharacteristic perverseness as much as real need. He stuck his head out of the tent's opening and called to the nearest guard.

The stocky soldier, hardly older than Kellen himself, and with a face only a mother would have kind words about, walked toward him. "Do you need something, my lord?" His tone was respectful and his expression professional.

Kellen regretted his churlish notions of the boy. "Would you please tell the baron's squire, Frederic, that I am in need of him?"

"Of course, my lord. I'll send him in to you."

This was a polite way of ordering Kellen back inside the tent. He complied because he didn't want to cause the soldier any trouble. He didn't have long to wait, anyway.

Frederic raced in. "Can I be of assistance, my lord?"

"I need the privy. Will you escort me there?"

"Certainly." The boy stood to one side to let Kellen go first. Once outside, he then led the way while sticking to Kellen's side. The squire didn't try to physically take hold of him in any manner, but he was a strong boy, learning the art of warfare. If he and Kellen tussled, Kellen had no doubt who would prevail, not that he wanted to cause him any trouble. Frederic had been kind to him.

Kellen felt the constraints nevertheless and wasn't oblivious to the curious stares of the soldiers along the way. Their attention on him was brief, and no one made any disrespectful or lewd gesture or remark. He supposed that was all due to the high regard, if not fear, of their leader.

The privy was surprisingly well-maintained and relatively private. He wasn't the only one using it, but everyone gave each other and him proper space. And there were buckets of fresh water and sponges to clean himself afterward. It was all quite civilized, and he was grateful for it. Although he'd never been on a military campaign himself, he'd heard stories that led him to believe it was a dirty, nasty affair, even outside of the battlefields. Maybe it was only his father's soldiers who camped under those conditions.

It was on his way back to the tent that he saw the baron not too far from him. He stumbled at the sight, unnerved more than frightened. He righted himself within seconds and set his gaze elsewhere, yet his face was heated with embarrassment. Only Frederic could have seen his reaction, and even then, the squire might not have appreciated the cause of it.

His hope died the moment they entered the tent.

"The baron is quite magnificent, is he not? I don't think there's a man in the whole of Moorcondia who is as big and handsome as he is."

Kellen scowled. "I hadn't noticed."

Frederic grinned. "Now, my lord, I think you're not being entirely honest about that."

Wilfred would have backhanded the boy for his impudence, but Kellen had never been able to bring himself to even verbally rebuke anyone. He turned away so Frederic couldn't see his expression. "I suppose you're irked over my having replaced you in Roth's bed." His words were said more out of a ridiculous and unwanted spurt of jealousy than insult at being called a liar.

The squire had the impudence to chuckle.

Kellen whipped his head around. "Are you denying it?"

"Of course, my lord. I don't warm the baron's bed. He would never take advantage of his power over me in such a way. Besides, I fancy girls, as he well knows — not that I've had the chance to dally with any." His expression turned pensive. "If we are to winter here, I am hoping to maybe meet a girl in town."

"Any girl who welcomes your advances will probably do so out of fear that she has no choice." Kellen didn't say it unkindly, but it was true, and

Frederic seemed a decent enough boy and needed to hear it."

Frederic nodded. "That's what the baron has said. I must tread carefully."

Kellen found himself being sucked into the boy's dilemma without meaning to. It was nice to converse with someone closer to his own age. Aside from the nuns, he had no friends. His father's contempt of him had discouraged anyone from trying to be kind, let alone grow close to him. "Surely there are camp followers you could visit."

"Yes." Frederic sighed and started straightening the tent, even though little was out of order. He picked up the book Kellen had read and placed it back where it belonged. "The thing is, I want a nice girl who likes me for myself, not for my coin. Someone I can perhaps marry who would want me as her husband." He shrugged. "I'm not merely looking for a place to stick my dick in."

"Nor should you." The baron strode into the tent. He jerked his head toward the tent flap. "Off you go, Frederic. We won't need you until supper time."

With a quick, shallow bow, the squire hurried from the tent.

"He's a good lad," Roth said. "One can't help but admire his dogged determination to make sex count emotionally and not only physically. I doubt you'd find anyone else in this camp with those kinds of scruples. I don't suppose you could put in a good word with one of the village girls...?"

Kellen inwardly shook himself out of the frozen state the baron's entry had caused. "I'm afraid not, and for no other reason than I don't know any — unless you count the nuns, that is," he added almost under his breath. Honestly, the stupid things that were coming out of his mouth since his capture.

The baron chuckled as he took off his cloak and tossed it onto a chest. Then he removed his sword belt and placed it on top of the cloak before going to pour himself a glass of wine. "Yes, let's not count the good sisters." He gestured toward the decanter. "Would you care for a glass?"

Kellen shook his head. "No thank you. I never drink before supper, unless it's to test a batch at the winery." Feeling awkward, he clasped his hands behind his back and went to study the array of books lined up on a free-standing case. "Do you always bring so much to read, or were you expecting a long siege?" It was a provocative question, reminding the man of why he was stuck in what was now a field of cold mud, waiting for large amounts of snow to make everything even more miserable.

The baron wandered over to the sitting area by the brazier and took the chair next to the one Kellen had occupied not so long ago. He relaxed into the seat, stretching his long legs in front of him and crossing his ankles. Even in such a pose, the man looked ready to spring up at any moment and wage battle with anyone who dared to attack him.

Kellen was *not* that man. Instead, he removed his own cloak and draped it over the other chair. He sat down, trying to convey more ease than he felt.

Roth took another sip of his wine before saying, "I always have some number of books, if only one. Most of those, however, Frederic bought for me at the bookseller's in the village. I haven't had a chance to read more than one or two. Did you enjoy the one I gave you this afternoon?"

Kellen wanted to spit out a vehement and dismissive denial, yet he simply didn't have it in him to be so churlish. "I did, yes. I don't know much about my own birthplace, it seems. My father doesn't like reading, so there aren't many books in Highrock." He felt as if he were betraying some secret of his family's by saying so. Still, it was something of a relief to speak the truth to someone who liked reading as much as he did.

"You had tutors, surely?"

Kellen's cheeks warmed at the question. It embarrassed him to reveal some truths because they were so painful. He answered anyway. The baron just seemed like a safe person to talk to, which was ridiculous, but still that's how he felt. "No, I didn't...have any," he clarified. "My nurse taught me how to read and some math. I learned the rest on my own." He shrugged. "I'm not an important part of my family. That's no lie or exaggeration. You possess no leverage in me."

The baron tossed back the rest of his wine before putting his glass on the table. He rose and walked behind Kellen, then put his hands on his shoulders.

Kellen stiffened with alarm, trying to dismiss how nice the touch felt and worried where it might lead. He practically held his breath as he waited to see what the man intended to do.

"I can only reassure you that I don't intend to try to use you as some kind of leverage." He pressed his fingers into Kellen's muscles. "You are so obviously tense. Let me help you relax. I hate that I have contributed to your anxiety."

The sincerity of the words was hard to argue against. As a matter of survival, Kellen was able to detect meaning behind words and expressions. He had learned to catch a lie and distrust pretty words and inviting smiles. He knew predators when he met them, and Baron Roth simply didn't ring any of the warning bells so finely honed within him. Under the gentle massage the man gave him, he forced himself to loosen his shoulders and close his eyes. No one had ever done this kindness for him before, although he'd seen servants do it—and more—for soldiers sitting around the great hall. Images of people kneeling between men's legs and taking their cocks into their mouths popped up before he could suppress them. His own dick thickened, and a moan passed his lips before he could stop it.

The baron stilled his fingers for a moment before continuing. "Feels good, doesn't it? And don't be alarmed at any reaction it elicits. The gods made us to want and need touch from others. I'm only sorry you seem to have received precious little of it in your life."

Tears pricked under Kellen's eyelids. "I don't want you to pity me." He hated that his voice shook some.

Roth's reply was given in a soft voice. "I can't help it, but if it makes you feel better, there are a lot more emotions I have for you. A *lot* more."

Chapter Five

Henry stared at the chessboard, his mind more on his rather foolish escapades earlier in the day with his guest than on figuring out his next move. Part of him wanted to apologize for the effrontery of putting his hands on Kellen and revealing more of his interest in the boy than he had intended to. It had simply been too much of a temptation to ease the boy's nerves, and naturally it had also been a huge rationalization for touching Kellen. There could be two things that were true at the same time, he reminded himself. It was unbearably sad to know that Cragmore had neglected his son to such a degree. How anyone could look at Kellen and not see the glory in him was mystifying…and infuriating. It made him wish for the opportunity to meet the man in battle, which was ridiculous. Whatever else the man was, he had fathered the boy, and children had a way of clinging to their parents emotionally, no matter what. How would Kellen feel about him if he killed his father?

It wouldn't inspire him to jump into my bed. Of that, Henry was certain. As little time as he'd spent in the boy's company, he was sure Kellen was not someone who would be indifferent toward, let alone pleased with, the man who'd killed his father.

"You are distracted I think, my lord baron." Kellen's expression was unreadable.

"Am I? I wonder why?" Regardless of his regret from the impromptu massage and provocative statement, he simply was incapable of reining himself in, apparently.

As he reached for a piece, Colin raced into the tent, tense and grim. "Hal, we have a problem that requires your immediate attention."

All thoughts of the game and Kellen fled at his man's expression and tone. He jumped to his feet and went to his chest. "I'm coming." He reached for his cloak and threw it over his shoulders. Without thinking why, he went to fetch Kellen's. "You come too?"

It was obvious the boy wanted to question it or refuse outright, Instead, he allowed Henry to drape the cloak over his shoulders and followed him out.

The air among his men as he strode beside Colin was thick with worry, every man on alert, but not in a way that came while readying for a battle. This was internal trouble, and whatever it was, Henry would deal with it swiftly to quell any concern or hint that good order was falling apart.

Gathered at the edge of camp was the obvious problem. A young soldier whom Henry didn't recognize was being held by both arms by two men he did know, one being Sir Hugh. Nearby was a tearful young woman, wrapped in what had to be her mother's embrace and a man he pegged as her father stood on her other side with fists clenched at his side.

Henry stopped between the two groups. "What has happened?"

Colin gestured toward the girl. "Mistress Anne claims that Spearman Alric here accosted her in the street as she walked home this evening and only released her when her father came in answer to her cries."

"She's lying," Alric sneered. "She wanted me until her old man showed up, then she claimed rape."

Henry turned a cold eye on the soldier. "Your opinion was not requested." Pleased when his gaze caused the man to shut his mouth and look away, Henry took a few steps closer to the weeping girl. Even in the gloom of torches and at a fair distance, he had no trouble seeing the torn collar of her gown and the bruises rising to the surface of her skin on either side of her neck. He didn't need to question her to know the truth.

He held his hand out in Colin's direction. The man knew what he wanted and plopped a fat purse in his upturned palm. That was one of the great things about his bannerman... Colin always thought ahead and knew his mind as well as he did.

Henry got close enough to the girl to hold out the purse. "Mistress Anne, please accept this token of my sincere apology and promise that this will never happen again." He made sure everyone understood he was giving it to her, the injured one, and not to her parents. It wasn't anything that was truly going to help her get past the horrific insult Alric had visited upon her, but it was the best he could do.

The girl hesitated a moment before sniffing back her tears and reaching out to take the purse. She hugged it to her chest. "W-will he be punished?" she dared to ask.

Admiring her courage, Henry gave her what he hoped was a reassuring smile. "Oh yes, he will. That I promise as well."

The girl nodded and let her mother lead her away. The father stayed as he was, though. "I want to watch." The man spat out his words, his anger unmollified by coin.

Letting an outsider witness punishment of a soldier was unorthodox, but Henry saw the wisdom of it. This man would report back to others in the village that the king's army took their complaints seriously and imposed discipline.

"Very well."

Behind him, Alric sputtered in outrage. "I've done nothing wrong, my lord. That—"

Henry spun on his heel, his furious gaze shutting the man up once more. "You really want to stop talking now." He looked at Colin. "Ready him. I'll be there in a moment." Turning back to the villager, he said. "Follow my man, if you please."

It was then that he remembered Kellen stood by. He'd insisted on the boy coming, but now he wanted him back in his tent, safe from the cold and the sight of what he was about to do.

The boy was clever enough to know his thinking. "You're not going to tell me to return to the tent, are you?"

"You aren't going to want to see the punishment I'm going to impose on that asshole. It's no more appropriate for you to watch than it is for that poor girl."

"I'm sure you're right. I've never shared my family's enjoyment of other's suffering. But like that girl's father, I think I need to see it. You said you would treat the village and the nuns fairly. I've seen some of that promise fulfilled already. You've been generous with my father's people, but it's just as important for me to know you mean to keep your men in check."

Henry was convinced that it was a bad idea to bring the boy along. Kellen probably assumed he'd be witnessing some enforcer meting out the punishment. He had no idea that Henry considered part of his duty to do whatever he would be willing to order someone else to. Still, it was cold, and the night wasn't going to get better on any level. He didn't want to stand there and argue any more, nor did he intend to have men drag the boy away. If he was to gain any amount of Kellen's trust, he had to persuade, not bully, him.

"Come then."

He walked purposely, yet unhurried, to the whipping post. It was a standard part of any camp, although he prided himself on not needing it much. Most of the soldiers ending up here took only a few strikes for minor offenses, sufficient to remind them to make better decisions. This matter, however, was a grave offense. Alric was lucky that Henry wasn't going to execute him over it.

Alric was already stripped to the waist and tied to the post by the time he and Kellen arrived. The girl's father stood to the side with Colin, who would be sure to stop the man if he decided to get some licks in himself. This was punishment, not retribution. Order had to be maintained. Knowing him well, the taskmaster handed over the coiled bullwhip once Henry was close.

Henry snapped it to its full length, grimly pleased when the offender shuddered. The guy had at least learned to keep his mouth shut.

"Spearman Alric, you have been found guilty of the crime of assault with intent to rape. I, Henry, Baron Roth, and your liege lord, sentence you to forty lashes and banishment back to your family in dishonor."

He let the crowd gathered absorb the pronouncement, knowing that he had given the limit under law that fell short of execution. It was as harsh as he could make it, intended to send a clear message to his men in case anyone was left doubting him on the issue of their conduct during the siege. Those who had fought with him before knew to behave. This was really a demonstration to the others.

Alric shuddered again and turned his face to look at him. "You *fucker!*"

Henry responded coldly. "You should never have put your hand around that girl's neck. You're lucky I don't break yours," he added before stepping into position.

He'd done this before, sad to say. Whipping was strenuous work, and one had to have a strong arm and the determination to carry out all of the lashes without pause. It didn't help the one delivering the punishment, nor the one receiving it, to drag the whole thing out. At first Alric stayed silent, pride making him think that he gave up something if he cried out. The pain overrode his stoicism after the tenth lash. Henry laid the stripes in even strokes to cover the man's back. With each lash, the whip cut deep. That was its purpose, after all. Blood was drawn, oozing from where the skin broke, then spraying into the air as the many strokes started to overlap.

Henry blocked out the sight of the carnage he wreaked and the sound of the man's suffering. He delivered the necessary strokes as quickly and as accurately as he could, ignoring the ache of his arm that screamed for a rest. The soldiers who stood in witness murmured among themselves, but there was no jeering. He didn't tolerate that kind of baiting of the offender. It took away from the solemnity of an act carried out as a matter of the king's justice. When he was done, his arm hung loosely from the exertion, and he felt slightly nauseous. He wasn't a man who took pleasure in the pain of others.

No one said anything now, the only sound being Alric's hitched breaths. Henry handed the whip over to the taskmaster. "See to the rest, Colin." He tried to keep the weariness from his voice and believed he failed.

"Yes, my lord. Cut him down," Colin barked.

Henry took the time to nod to the villager, seeing satisfaction on the man's face. Then he made his way back to his tent as quickly as he could. The sound of footsteps hurrying to keep up with him was the only reminder that his unwilling guest had remained with him. *What does Kellen think of me now?* Surely the duke's son saw him as a man every bit as vicious as his father. For some reason, the thought of it stung in a way that wasn't about extracting information from the boy.

"Brandywine, Frederic!" he barked as he pushed into the tent. His squire was way ahead of him, holding out a glass and with a decanter of the strong liquor on the table. Henry took the drink. "Good lad. Go to bed."

He gulped down half the glass as he tossed his cloak off and before throwing himself into the chair by the brazier. He stared moodily into the low flame, waiting for the liquor to kick in.

"You were kind."

Henry glanced at Kellen as the boy joined him by sitting in the other chair. His cloak was folded neatly, and he laid it on his lap. "That's a ridiculous observation, given that I just stripped a man's skin off his back."

Kellen ran his palm along the fur collar of his cloak. "You were quick and efficient. You didn't drag it out, tormenting the man, nor did you give him a fatal number of lashes. My father, who never bothers to lift his own hand for strenuous and dirty work, orders a hundred when he is particularly mad at the offender. They either live or die from that many strokes. He doesn't care one way or another." He gazed at Henry. "And he wouldn't have cared what that girl said. His men can do as they like, so long as they leave whomever my father is lying with at the moment alone. And that's only because she belongs to him—and no one touches his property without his permission."

Henry drained his glass and rose to get more. "I abhor men preying on women. My rules are very clear on the subject. Good order has to be maintained, and we can't afford to make enemies of the villagers." He started for his chair, then stopped to grab the decanter. There was no point in having to get up every time to refill his glass. "Besides all that, I believed her."

"It still matters that you cared. Most powerful men don't."

Henry merely shrugged and stared into his glass.

"And you didn't delegate the nasty task to someone else. You're wielding the whip yourself was...remarkable."

Irritated at the way Kellen seemed to be admiring him, he glared at the boy. "I'm just a good leader, that's all. I do what needs to be done, no matter how unpleasant. Now, if you don't mind, I prefer to drop the subject and work on getting drunk. Go to bed," he added before draining his glass once more.

"I...don't think that's wise—the getting drunk part."

"To bed! Unless you want to distract me from this evening's unpleasantness another way?" He gave this obvious suggestion with as much as a leer as he could, pushing aside how he sounded no better than Alric had acted.

Kellen rose with a sniff. "If you prefer the company of Brandywine to talking to me, have at it. I won't be offering any solace other than someone to talk to who isn't your subordinate."

Hating how he was wearing his feelings on his sleeve, Henry couldn't resist pushing the boy away. "No, you're not my subordinate. You're something even more inappropriate for me to spill my thoughts to—my prisoner." He winced inwardly at his harsh words. The drink was already loosening his tongue in terrible ways. The truth was, it embarrassed him that his thoughts and feelings were so obvious to the boy. "I don't need your pity or your approval, no more than you say you want mine. Go to bed, Kellen. I'm not fit company. But I'm also no threat to you," he added when the boy headed for the bed.

Kellen looked at him from over his shoulder. "Oh, I trust you on that, my lord. You strike me as a leader who applies the same standard of conduct for his troops to himself. Who would wield the whip when it's you in need of punishment?"

You. Henry nearly said it out loud. The boy's expression and cutting words were drawing plenty of blood as it was. Turning to his drink, he blocked Kellen from mind and got busy with the work of getting blind drunk.

* * * *

Henry didn't want to wake to his pounding head and dry mouth. It was far nicer to remain right where he was, snuggled beneath his covers and holding a body against his chest. It was something new and amazing to clasp such soft, smooth skin. As his mind slowly came around to full consciousness, his first thought was he'd never had such a lovely bedmate. His second thought was...*Kellen*.

"Shit!" Henry rolled away so quickly he went right over his side of the bed and landed on the floor of his tent with a jarring thump. The impact made his head feel as if it were falling off. He wasn't so hungover, though, to miss his rampant erection standing tall and demanding attention. Grabbing the edge of the comforter, he covered his lap, then ran a hand through his disheveled hair to tame it, as if his appearance mattered somehow.

Kellen slid over to the edge of the bed and lay on his side with his head resting on his palm. "Good morning, Baron."

Henry blinked hard at the boy. "I...ah, please accept my sincere apology, my lord. I was unaware of my actions last night."

Kellen smirked. "Oh, I know that. And you were so far into your cups, that thing," he said, pointing at Henry's lap, "was little more than an old, limp carrot all night. As far as I'm concerned, you acted as nothing other than an extra blanket—one that stunk of Brandywine," he added with a look of disgust.

Henry was at a loss for words, an unusual occurrence for him. He'd been a bore and, apparently, a pathetic drunk. It was so unlike him. He would have put it down to the long siege and his distaste for whipping a man bloody, but it was really more than that if he were being honest with himself. Kellen had burrowed in under his skin, and his inability to resist the boy was turning him into an idiot.

There was a scratching at the tent flap and before Henry could formulate a reply, Colin sauntered in with a tankard in his hand and a grin on his face. "Good morning, Hal. I have just what you need." So saying, he came over and handed him the drink.

Henry didn't hesitate to take the tankard and downed its vile contents in one long swallow. Experience told him it would do the trick to ease his head and queasy stomach. He just had to override his taste buds.

Colin watched with obvious glee. "And how are you, Lord Kellen?" he asked, slipping his gaze to the bed.

"Well enough, thank you, Sir Colin," the boy replied with a certain amount of primness. He was covered still by the comforter but only to the waist so all that creamy, white skin of his chest was on full display.

Henry had the urge to cover Kellen up to his chin. Instead, he wiped the hangover cure from his lips and handed the tankard over to Colin. "Hand me my trousers."

Colin made a show of looking around for them. "You mean these?" With his forefinger and thumb, he lifted the garment off the decanter—the completely empty one—and passed it over to Henry.

Henry snatched them from his friend's hand. "Thank you." He wiggled them on under the cloth that was doing a poor job of hiding his erection. The tightness of getting his trousers past his hard dick made him wince.

Colin picked up the empty decanter and studied it. "Impressive." He went to put it on the table. "You take these things too much to heart, Hal. The boy got what he deserved."

Hating how Colin was reading him so correctly in front of Kellen, he stood quickly and was amazed he didn't fall onto his ass, given how much the tent spun. He tied the laces to his trousers with a grimace. "What's his status?"

"Alric spent the night in the medic's tent. The doctor says he can leave for home in a day or two. I've already assigned two guards to make sure he arrives, and the full story of his dishonor is provided to his family. Put him from your mind. I've got this."

Henry merely grunted. He knew Colin had everything well in hand, took his advice about putting the fucking spearman out of his thoughts and turned his attention to the boy in his bed. "You should get dressed, Lord Kellen. Frederic will be here shortly with our breakfast." He focused his attention on his stomach for a moment and was able to confirm he was hungry. Colin's miraculous concoction worked fast.

Kellen didn't exactly leap to obey him, but he did throw off the comforter and started to rise. The boy was wearing only his smallclothes, the emphasis being *small*. Through the thin cotton, the outline of Kellen's slender cock was visible. His ass was high and tight, while his limbs were supple. No hair graced his thin chest, and Henry was surprised to realize how attractive it was. He usually appreciated his bed partners' hairiness, not having much himself. The boy's long, blond hair cascaded down his back almost to his narrow waist. Really, he was exquisite. Henry simply had to learn to ignore the inappropriate attraction to his guest and get on with the true purpose of keeping him close.

When Kellen bent over to retrieve the rest of his clothing, his rump became an impossible sight to turn away from, until Henry realized that Colin was also staring in that direction.

"Get out, Colin."

The man had the audacity to smirk. "Why? Frederic is bringing my breakfast here, as well. We're going over the accounts, remember?"

Damnation! "Turn around, then." Henry recognized that his words were those of a jealous man, yet he couldn't stop himself.

Colin simply sighed and did as he was told — and so did Henry. He no more had the right to stare at Kellen's alluring backside than his bannerman did. Fortunately for them both, Frederic came in, carrying a big, heavy tray of breakfast for three.

Henry only managed to pull on his socks and boots and throw yesterday's shirt over himself before going to sit. Kellen was on his way to the table, too, and they intersected before arriving there. There was one of those idiotic social dances that happened when two people tried to avoid each other and kept doing the opposite. A few feints occurred before Henry gave vent to his frustration and his desire by grabbing Kellen by the waist and lifting him. He set the boy down by his chair where he belonged before taking his own seat. Kellen had let out a gasp of surprise at the touch, but otherwise said nothing. He sat and flicked his napkin onto his lap as if nothing had happened.

Henry admired the boy's ability to hide his emotions, a skill no doubt mastered from childhood growing up in the duke's castle. Kellen was better at it than he was, much as he tried to not react to the shocking warmth that had spread from his fingertips right down to his cock. Such a simple touch and yet it was the most provocative thing that had happened to him in…forever.

Focusing on his own meal, Henry pretended that he felt nothing. Colin's expression told him he wasn't succeeding. "Shut up," he ordered his bannerman. Then he accepted the plate Frederic handed him.

Colin's eyes went wide. "I didn't say anything, my lord."

Henry narrowed his gaze, aware that their interaction was being observed by the boys. "Shut up anyway." With that warning, he speared a piece of sausage and stuffed it into his mouth.

Chapter Six

Kellen had forgotten the simple, yet fantastic pleasure of taking a bath until he sank down in the tub up to his shoulders. The good sisters didn't go in for such luxury, and since his capture, he'd only been afforded sponge baths, which he'd accomplished as quickly as possible, aware that he'd been exposed to the baron's disconcerting gaze. The water was warm and fragrant, something decidedly masculine like sandalwood. With his eyes closed, he could almost believe he was back in his own chambers in the castle, shut away from the raucous denizens, and free to imagine he was somewhere better, safer.

But he wasn't alone. The baron lay in a tub beside him, his big body fitting only up to his waist, leaving everything above it—chest and wide shoulders, thickly muscled arms—on display. That was a distraction he couldn't block out, no matter where he looked. It had been hard enough to keep from staring at the man as they'd disrobed. The tent was ample for its task of functioning as a place for bathing yet had been far too small for him to ignore his captor. Roth was a perfect man, as far as Kellen was concerned. There wasn't a part of him that was unappealing to someone who coveted men. The man sported just enough hair on his chest for one to twine a finger or two and a treasure trail led to an impressively large cock—both long and thick. Fully aroused, it would be a hard thing to take anywhere in one's body. Still, it made him shudder with unseemly delight at the prospect.

He knew how it felt, too, when it was hard. He'd lied to the baron earlier when he'd mocked him as being too drunk during the night to become erect. When the man had wrapped his arms around Kellen from behind, his hard length had pressed against the cleft of Kellen's ass—not menacing, simply there. It should have frightened him to be in a man's embrace without invitation. If the baron had been inclined, he would have easily overpowered him. There would have been nothing he could have done to stop his captor if he'd rolled Kellen onto his stomach, covered his body and… *Best not to think about it.* If he didn't focus on something else, his own dick would rise, regardless of where he was, with four servants bustling about, stoking the brazier and adding hot water to the tubs as the water started to cool. The embarrassment would kill him.

Sinking lower into the water, his knees popping up because of the shortness of the tub, Kellen tried to remind himself that Roth was his enemy, his captor, someone he should be wary of, even if he couldn't muster up any hatred for the man. The baron was only doing the king's bidding, after all, and Kellen had no interest in his father's foolish quest to declare the North as his own fiefdom. In fact, far from being afraid the previous night, the baron's embrace had made him feel oddly safe. For the first time in his life, Kellen had been entirely unafraid that something bad might happen. There was no fear that his brother would barge into his room, demanding he do some manly task, then mocking him when he couldn't measure up. There was no worry, as there had been at the nunnery, that soldiers would descend on the peaceful place and wreak havoc out of a dubious sense of duty or just out of spite. No, Roth's body was like an impenetrable shield against danger. Kellen had slept truly peacefully. The experience puzzled him. For sure, though, he no longer feared being the baron's captive. It was easy to relax in the warm water with his eyes closed.

"I have duties to attend to that will last most of the day."

The sudden sound of the man's voice caused Kellen's eyes to fly open. He sat straighter in the tub and slid his gaze sideways. "Oh? You need not explain your movements to me." He stared across the tent in front of him, but no longer felt languid enough to close his eyes again.

There was the sound of sloshing water. Kellen told himself not to look, but he did anyway. The sight of Roth was too compelling to resist. The man had risen from his bath. He stepped out, his golden skin dripping with water. A servant handed him a towel.

Roth rubbed the cloth across his chest. "Perhaps not, but I wouldn't want you to think I'd forgotten about you." The man dared to grin as he proceeded to wipe down his arms.

Kellen jerked his gaze away again. "I assure you, Baron, that your company will not be missed."

"Ah, now, once again, you've wounded my pride, Lord Kellen." The man shook his head like a dog, droplets of water flying from his short hair. Then he made quick work of drying his back and legs before striding over to where a fresh set of clothing lay. The change in location put him in Kellen's line of sight.

Now it was impossible to avoid watching him as he rubbed dry his genitals, making his cock and balls swing. Then he bent over to attend to his feet, giving Kellen a good look at his muscular ass. All Kellen could think of was how that powerful part of him would be able to drive his dick hard and fast into... Kellen slammed his eyelids shut, working to keep his breath even and placing his hands across his groin to make sure his dick behaved. He hoped that his warming cheeks would be put down to the steam rising from the water.

"I'm sure the thousands of people in this camp who hang on your every word and deed will help soothe whatever hurt I may have caused." Kellen knew better than to bait a powerful person but couldn't help himself. It was his only defense against his own inappropriate reaction to his captor.

His impudence was met with a chuckle. "If ever my head gets too big, I know where to go to right-size it." There was rustling as the man dressed. "Frederic will see you back to my tent and bring you your lunch. Make yourself at home and feel free to read whatever books you find. If nothing strikes your fancy, I dare say Frederic can scrounge up others."

Kellen didn't trust his voice, so he said nothing. And he kept his eyes closed, even as he heard the baron leave the tent. He stayed in the tub until the water cooled and refused an offer from a boy to add more. His skin had already wrinkled, and it wasn't fair to take up space when there must be others in need of a bath.

When a servant tried to rub him dry, he demurred, taking the towel himself. He really didn't like anyone touching him, *except for the baron, apparently*. That reaction to the man was still a puzzle. Worse, he couldn't help looking forward to the night to come. It was perverse, and yet there it was.

He used the comb someone handed him to detangle, then braid his hair. The long strands were a part of himself that gave him pride. He'd noticed, too, that the baron seemed fixated on it, probably because it was so opposite of the color of his own. That thought also perversely pleased him. *I must stop thinking about that man!*

Someone had freshened up his clothing, so he didn't mind putting them back onto his clean body. Frederic appeared to lead him back to the baron's tent. He left Kellen with a bowl of dried fruit to snack on and a promise that he would come running if Kellen asked one of the guards stationed outside to fetch him. The tent felt oddly empty now with no one there but him. Only a day ago, he'd have relished the idea of being left alone. Now, he felt…restless.

Taking the baron at his word, Kellen poked around the books the man kept. There were papers and record books of some sort or another lying about, as well. He was tempted to look through them but decided that would be a waste of time. It didn't matter what they were or the information they might contain. This siege was only his business in as much as he was the traitorous duke's son. He actually wanted it to end as quickly as possible, his only real concern being that none of the innocent people in the castle would be killed. The whole thing was pointless—the outcome clear to anyone with sense. And it was stupid. Auden was a good king as far as Kellen could tell, fair and no tyrant. Only rank hunger for power was the reason for the rebellion.

He picked a book on building bridges to read. It was an intriguing choice of topic for a soldier to have and not one he would have thought interested him. Sitting in what he'd come to think of already as 'his chair', he became absorbed in the narrative of buttresses and trusses. Drawings of each stage of construction made it easy to follow. Before he knew it, it was time for lunch. Frederic laid out thick pieces of hearty oat bread, thin slices of meat and shavings of cheese. There was a tangy salad of the season's last tomatoes mixed with bitter greens. The squire set down a large jug of cool cider. And not surprisingly, there was dessert, as well — small spice cakes with a thick layer of buttery frosting on top. The king's men ate better on their campaign than most villagers did — or maybe it was only he who was being pampered so. It might all be a clever ploy of the baron to loosen Kellen's tongue. No matter. He wasn't going to turn down the delicious food. There was only one piece of valuable information that he could provide to his captor, but no amount of treats was going to loosen his tongue. The one skill he was good at in addition to making wine was keeping his mouth shut.

Kellen returned to his chair to continue reading, cakes and cider by his side. The book was so technical in nature that it absorbed his concentration and took him much longer to get through than others. Once more, he lost track of time, so was startled when the baron came striding in. The man looked as if he'd worked up a sweat, his hair appearing darker and his face shiny. Without ceremony, the man removed his cloak and his shirt, then splashed water on his face, neck and underarms from a basin that Frederic had hurried to bring in.

The baron wiped a cloth over his dripping skin and eyed Kellen. "Keeping yourself amused, my lord?" Before Kellen could muster up a reply, the man turned his attention to his squire. "That was a good effort, Frederic."

The boy was also visibly sweaty. "Thank you, my lord. You were right about it being easier to fight in the cold, even with the extra layer of clothing. I hadn't appreciated how much heat bogs you down."

The baron nodded as he accepted a clean shirt from Frederic. "Yes, I could tell that your arm swung with greater ease. But that's also a function of how much muscle you've put on since the beginning of the summer season. In a few more years, your body will have filled out into manhood. Those soldiers your age who are bloodied in battle already are experienced, but the hard truth is they are expendable, and you're destined to lead. It's important that you do so well-trained and fully grown."

The squire blushed with obvious appreciation. "Yes, my lord. I'll see to your supper after I bathe."

"No rush," the baron replied as he pulled the shirt over his head. His attention returned to Kellen. "Do you fancy a game of chess before we dine?"

Kellen tried not to blush like Frederic had under Roth's scrutiny and shrugged. "I suppose so. I'm finished with this book anyway." Putting it aside, he rose and joined the baron at the table.

Roth set up the chessboard, and as usual, he gave the white pieces to Kellen.

He made his first move almost without thinking, putting a pawn forward, then leaned his jaw against his upturned palm. "We don't even think about sacrificing these pawns, do we? Much like those peasant boys out there risking their lives to better themselves and in an effort to support those who rule over them."

Roth poured himself a cup of water and drank it down as he made his move. Crossing his arms, he propped his elbows on the tabletop. "I suppose not. Everyone has their place in an orderly world, do they not? And sacrifice for the greater good is never a wasted effort."

Kellen merely grunted before moving his next piece.

Roth studied the board. "Chess is an informative example of society. Here we have a king and queen, rulers with power, to be safeguarded as much as possible, with even the queen willing to sacrifice herself to protect the king. Then we have those that serve them and help keep order—bishops and nights, and these somewhat enigmatic rooks that wield great power anyway, and yes, even the pawns." He made his move. "They all serve toward a single purpose, and while we always start out with two sides, in the end, only one is left standing." He flicked his gaze at Kellen. "It's a good outcome, don't you think? If there were no victor, conflict would never end and all these pieces would have to continue to endlessly move, getting knocked out over and over again. Worse yet, a draw means that no one can gain the upper hand, leaving everyone frozen, neither side moving forward. No one benefits from that, either."

Kellen moved his knight before responding. "And yet, here we sit, playing the game again, not being satisfied with the last victory standing. It is the nature of people to want to try to achieve dominance over an opponent, not simply acquiescing to the other player's superiority. If your point was to make an analogy of chess with life, you've missed the mark. If anything, your eagerness to play with me again proves that my father's quest for victory is perfectly understandable, even if it is misguided. He can't win. I know that."

Roth captured one of Kellen's pawns and held it up, rubbing his thumb over its smooth surface. "You're right. If my intent was to try to convince you to help me end this siege, I've done a bad job of it. However," he added, placing the pawn to one side of the board, "this soldier is off the board only until the game ends. Then he is resurrected to live again. Not so for humans... If the average soldier out there gets cut down, he stays down, any chance of a good life gone forever. I'll force that sacrifice if I have to, but I prefer not to. Can you say the same about your father? Does he care about the loss of life his doomed quest for power will cost?"

Fury, fueled by impotence, erupted inside Kellen. He swept all of the pieces off the board with his hand and jumped to his feet. He paced away from the table, hugging himself, trying to quell the desire to cry and the shaking that came from keeping them at bay. "You ask too much of me. I can't help you!" Even as he cried out those words, he cringed inside, knowing that wasn't really true. But he had no way of knowing how any help he might give Roth would protect the people in the castle. He might cause their destruction.

He stopped by the brazier and stared into its low flames. He had to blink hard to keep the tears back. Then he jumped when arms came around his shoulder. He wanted to pull away from the baron's embrace yet couldn't manage it. Instead, he leaned into the man, seeking the same sense of safety that he'd felt during the night.

"I'm sorry. I didn't mean for our pastime to turn into an interrogation." The man's voice was low and soothing. "Well, that's not true. I did intend to pry information out of you, but I hadn't meant for it to upset you so."

"I'm not upset." Kellen had meant to firmly deny his emotional state. His watery voice belied that claim, however. And as much as his thoughts urged him to pull away, he melted into the baron's embrace. It was hardly comfortable. Everything about the man was hard, including his dick. The ridge of it pressed against the small of his back.

Roth rubbed his chin along the top of Kellen's head. "I'm sorry about that—the obvious proof of my arousal. I can't manage to keep it under control when I'm near you, let alone touching you."

When the man tried to pull away, though, Kellen perversely reached up to grasp his arms. "It's all right. I understand. And I can't say it bothers me. Not really. I don't have any sense, I guess. At least that's what my father and siblings have always said."

Roth tightened his grip for a moment, almost squeezing the breath out of Kellen. "They are fools—and not simply because of this ill-advised rebellion. Your value is obvious to anyone with eyes not blinded by ambition and too stupid to see beyond their own noses. If you need proof that you are worthy of respect and admiration, look no further than the good sisters and the villagers concerned with your welfare. If you were mine, Kellen, I would treat you like the precious person you are."

Kellen finally found the strength to pull away. After a moment of tightening his embrace, Roth let him go. "But I'm not yours." He turned to face the man. "Other than my mother when I was very young and she was still alive, my family has never shown me kindness. Wilfred's wife was a nice woman, but even she kept her distance, not wanting to catch her husband's ire. As bad as my father and sister have been, they're still my family, though. Don't expect me to betray them." It was as close to admitting he might have useful information as he'd gotten. He stood staring at Roth, pleading with his eyes for the man to let it go.

The baron stared back, then blowing out a breath, he said, "You're right. I won't try to pry information out of you anymore. Shall we return to the chessboard and start again?" He shook his head. "No, I can see that it's too soon for that. How about we just sit quietly and read?"

When Kellen nodded, Roth went to his small library and picked out two books. He handed one to Kellen. "I think you'll like this. It's a story about a boy following his older sister on a dangerous yet noble quest. It has a happy ending," he added with a quick smile.

Kellen smiled shyly back at him and took the book. "Thank you. It sounds like something I'd like, even though I'd never follow Isolde anywhere—not that she'd want me to."

They sat in their respective chairs with the brazier between them, each reading and looking like a comfortable married couple enjoying some quiet time together. It was an image that Kellen wasn't used to, but he thought it all the same. It didn't bother him, either, and that was a surprise. And it wasn't as scary as it should have been that he'd grown comfortable in the baron's company so quickly. Had it really been only a couple of days since his capture? *Why am I so content?* It wasn't rational, but it was true. There was no point in denying it or fighting against his own feelings. For the rest of the afternoon, he simply allowed himself to be free of worry and to lose himself in the story he read. Roth had been right. It was very enjoyable.

Frederic's sudden appearance, followed by Sir Colin, irritated Kellen. The presence of the two men shattered the illusion of he and the baron being alone in their own small world. Putting down his book, he worked to school his expression into one of indifference.

"Ah, our supper." Roth acted as if he were happy to see his squire and his bannerman, yet there was a small tightening around his mouth, as if he too was annoyed at the interruption. "Frederic, pick up the chess pieces and put them away. Lord Kellen and I tired of the game quickly."

Sir Colin lifted one brow as he looked around to where the pieces had scattered. "I'll say. Did you lose, Hal?"

"No." The baron frowned at the man before returning his book to its proper place.

Colin surprised Kellen by taking the chair the baron had vacated. "You know, my lord," he said leaning toward him and keeping his voice low, "I'm no competition to you. Baron Roth and I are merely old friends, nothing more. I'd say we were practically like brothers, but we've been known to indulge in activities siblings should not do with each other." He grinned.

Kellen grimaced before he could stop himself. "It's of no matter to me one way or another what you and Roth get up to. I'm his prisoner, remember?"

"Mmm. Yes, prisoners always dine with their captors, play chess with them, read by their side and...sleep in their beds."

Kellen narrowed his eyes. "None of that is my choice. The baron has made it clear that I must stay here with him, and while I do so, I may as well find enjoyable ways to pass the time."

The knight's expression sobered. "Yes, of course, my lord. That's all true, except if the situation truly bothers you, you might try putting up a ruckus over it all—you know, kicking, screaming, throwing things. I'm willing to bet the baron would have you hauled out to somewhere else if you did."

Before Kellen could muster up a reply, a bread roll bounced off Sir Colin's face.

"Behave yourself, old friend, or I'll have *you* removed from my tent." The baron's gaze shot from where he stood by the table was chilling.

The knight didn't appear fazed by the rebuke. He picked up the roll and took a bite out of it. As he chewed, he walked toward his lord. "I was only trying to help, Hal."

The baron wasn't appeased. "Like an archer with poor aim ends up shooting one of his fellow soldiers. It's hard to appreciate such a misguided attempt."

Sir Colin merely shrugged as he finished his roll and sat at the table.

Roth turned his attention to Kellen, his face morphing into one of kindness and patience. "Come and eat, my lord. I promise Sir Colin will behave himself."

Kellen rose with as much nonchalance as he could muster. "It doesn't matter to me what either of you say or do. I know my place."

The baron held his chair for him. "Yes, I'm rather afraid you do."

Before Kellen could make out the man's meaning, Roth sat and the meal began. It was a quiet affair, no one saying much. There was a tension between him and his captor, however, that made Kellen both dread and long for the night ahead. The conflicting feelings confused him, so instead of dwelling on them, he focused on his meal and pictured building a bridge in his head. It was distracting, yet not enough so that he could block out his host entirely. Every noise the man made skittered along his skin, and every move of his large, powerful hands made Kellen's spine tingle. As soon as the meal was finished, he made his excuses to retire early.

He shed his clothing with his back to the table and slid under the covers. He fell asleep to the soothing sound of the baron's voice as he talked to his bannerman. Kellen didn't question the why of his reaction now, though. What was the point? The baron had captured him in more than a physical way. He was truly trapped.

Chapter Seven

Henry woke to the sound of sleet hitting the tent. He nearly groaned at the realization that winter was threatening its arrival more earnestly. His men would be cranky with the nasty weather. Those that had tents would be bored from being cooped up to escape it. Colin was likely already implementing indoor training and skill-building games. Henry needed to get up and help him, show his men that nothing short of a full-blown blizzard should bog any army down. The only problem was he didn't want to get out of bed, especially as he was extra warm from having another body plastered against his own.

This time, it had been Kellen who had migrated across the expanse of mattress to cuddle. There was no other word for it. The boy embraced him from the back, one slender arm hung loosely over his waist while a head was tucked into the crook of shoulder. Henry's dick was as hard as iron from the touch. That wasn't surprising. No, the unexpected bit of this sleep-induced affection was that Kellen was also aroused. There was no other explanation for the hardness rubbing against his ass cheek.

It doesn't mean anything, just a biological response. He couldn't assume that just because Kellen had rolled over—and over again—in his sleep to hold him and had become aroused that it meant the boy actually wanted him. Henry was duty-bound to pull away and get up, trying to pretend it never happened. And yet, he couldn't quite banish from his memory the unmistakable sexual tension between them that had only been growing since he'd pulled off that habit to expose Kellen's identity. It wasn't merely wishful thinking, either. Colin's mortifying effort to reassure Kellen that Henry was fair game meant that his friend was aware of what was happening, too. *It's not my imagination.*

On a deep breath sucked in for courage, Henry rolled over to face Kellen. It was an incredibly risky thing to do, but Henry had to try it. If the boy woke, screaming bloody murder, Henry would have to find a new place to keep him confined. The temptation to make the boy his would be too great, and forcing himself on him even in small ways would be intolerable.

Kellen stirred, half awake. Although he stiffened for a moment, he didn't pull away. Instead, he cuddled closer, his warm breath tickling Henry's chest. Kellen's arm remained across Henry's waist, as well. Taking it all as a sign to continue, Henry clasped both hard cocks in one hand. The two shafts were very mismatched. Kellen's was significantly shorter and thinner than his own. Jerking them together was awkward at first, but he soon gained a rhythm. The boy began to pant, and his grip tightened on Henry's hip, small fingers digging into his skin. At the moment cum spurted onto Henry's fingers, Kellen let out a muted cry. Shudders racked his body, and when he was still again, Henry tried to release his dick in order to continue to find relief solo. But Kellen mewed with distress and grabbed his hand to keep it in place.

Henry smiled against the boy's head, ridiculously pleased at both the outcome and the desire on Kellen's part to keep them linked. It didn't take long for the boy's dick to harden again, and by the time Henry climaxed, Kellen was coming for a second time. Henry bucked into his own fist, mashing their bodies together and wringing out the last bit of cum. When it became painfully sensitive to keep pulling his cock, he let go, assuming Kellen was equally spent. He would have pulled away entirely, except once again, his captive-turned lover wouldn't let him.

"Is it okay if we stay like this for a while?"

Henry gave into the urge to kiss the top of Kellen's head. "Yes, of course. Are you...was that well-done of me? You aren't upset or afraid that you had no choice?"

"If I hadn't wanted it, I would have let you go the first time." He wiggled a hand between their bodies and twined a few strands of Henry' chest hair with a finger. "I thought of doing this while we bathed, even though I was embarrassed by my urges. There doesn't seem much point in denying what I want now." He tugged gently, playfully. "Am I hurting you?"

"No." *But you could, oh so easily.* Facing his own emotional vulnerability was hard, and getting involved with Kellen was a foolish thing to do. They were on opposite sides of this siege, and however it ended, the boy was probably going to hate him for what he did. At most, they had the winter to spend together. After that... "We should rise. Frederic will be here any moment."

"I don't care." The boy sighed. "I'm tired of being worried all the time. And keeping up the pretense of not being afraid or attracted to you is exhausting."

"You have nothing to fear from me." He dared to slide his cum-soaked hand across Kellen's hip and cup his ass. "I won't let anything bad happen to you."

"I know. Against any good sense, I trust you. And what others think of me doesn't matter. It never has. I'm no one of any importance or power."

Henry couldn't help squeeze the handful of flesh. "Don't say that. While it is true, you have no control over what is happening here generally, you aren't without influence, and you are very important. I would rather cut off my cock than have you feel like you have no agency over your own body."

"What you did was amazing. I don't regret it, and obviously some part of me wanted you to do something, because I migrated over to you. My sleeping self gave in to my deepest desires." He lifted his chin to look Henry in the eye. "I want more and everything else two men can do with each other. That doesn't mean I'll tell you anything to help break the siege, though," he added with an almost sorry expression.

"I won't ask you to do so." And just as Henry was considering giving in to Kellen's invitation and his own rising dick, Frederic came in, dripping wet.

The squire barely paused when he caught sight of them. He put his covered tray on the table before removing his cloak. "It's porridge today with lots of honey, dried fruit and nuts. Cook says with weather like this, it helps to have hearty food that sticks to your ribs."

Henry rose quickly to give Kellen more privacy. He broke the thin coating of ice on the washbowl and cleaned his hands of cum before splashing some of the freezing water into his face. "Freshen this," he ordered, holding the bowl toward his squire.

Frederic took it and without a question or complaint, threw his cloak back on and went out into the horrid weather once more.

"You didn't need to make him fetch clean water on my account. Most of the...mess landed on you." Kellen had slipped on his trousers, shirt and socks, leaving his lovely hair somewhat tangled down his back.

Henry walked over to him. "In my haste to indulge in carnal matters, I forgot something important." Clasping his hands behind his back, he leaned into the boy. "May I?"

Kellen blinked back at him, and for a moment, Henry feared he'd been too subtle. *Has no one ever kissed him?* Of course, they hadn't. The boy's upbringing could only be described as neglectful at best. The knowledge speared his heart, and he resolved to make him as happy as he could during the time they had together.

Just as Henry opened his mouth to ask for permission in a more pointed way, Kellen closed his eyes and pursed his lips. The gesture was adorable. Henry would teach the boy what kissing was all about later. For now, he brushed his mouth against Kellen's, the barest of contact, then pulled back. What he really wanted to do was take the boy in his arms and devour him, but that would be too much too soon. He needed to practice patience.

"Thank you, Kellen. I should have done that first instead of what I did do."

Kellen opened his eyes. "T-that's okay. I didn't expect you to. I've seen a lot of fucking in my father's castle and not much kissing." He lowered his gaze. "I assume it's of no real importance when seeking pleasure."

Henry lifted the boy's chin with his finger. "There is a great deal of pleasure to be had in a variety of ways. When my schedule permits and if you agree, I intend to show how much."

Kellen's cheeks pinked up. "I believe I'd like that."

The young lord proved so enticing that Henry considered beginning those lessons immediately. At that moment, however, Frederic returned, proving that the squire had a knack for being an undesirable chaperone.

"I've brought fresh water for you, Lord Kellen."

Kellen moved away from Henry and went over to the table. "Thank you, but I'll wash after breakfast. I don't mind it cooling off, and this food is best eaten hot."

And because it was both true about the porridge and wise to let go of his sexual impulse, Henry sat down to eat. The condiments made the gloppy stuff taste better, and the way that Kellen seemed to be enjoying the meal caused Henry to eat without much thought, anyway. It was pleasant to do something as ordinary as breaking one's fast when there was a pretty companion by one's side.

Kellen blushed some more as he stuck a few stray strands of his white-blond hair behind his ear. "You're staring at me, Baron." The admonishment in his voice was mild.

"I can't help it. You are much better-looking than the porridge."

Kellen rolled his eyes. "It's unseemly."

Henry refilled both of their cups with tea. "There's no one to notice except Frederic, and he doesn't mind."

Kellen sipped some of his tea before saying, "I'm not sure that's entirely true, but even if it is, it makes me uncomfortable."

Properly chastised, Henry changed his gaze to his bowl. "I apologize. It wasn't my intention to make you uncomfortable."

Kellen surprised him by putting one of his small hands on top of Henry's. "I'm new to this…this kind of attention. My thoughts and feelings are a jumble. Please be patient with me. I'm not sure what I want and need to sit with my thoughts for a while."

Henry nodded. "I understand and will honor your request. In this way, you are in charge."

"Thank you."

As soon as Kellen removed his hand, Henry missed the contact. Disturbed by his own free-wheeling emotions, he hastened to finish the meal.

"I'll be back for lunch," he said, grabbing his cloak, and didn't wait for a response.

He stepped out into the sleet and welcomed the chance for the cold to stifle his hot blood.

* * * *

"Honestly, Hal, I feel like a nursemaid, trying to keep our charges occupied and pacified to ward off a tantrum." Colin lifted his head to the sky. "At least the sleet has stopped. Gods, what is the point of it? Make up your mind, weather—rain or snow. Doing both at the same time is ridiculous."

Henry let his bannerman bitch and moan all the way to his tent. He welcomed the distraction, truth be told. All morning, he'd focused on the business of leading a large camp of soldiers and put aside how his day had begun with Kellen—mostly. Part of his mind was constantly dwelling on the boy. No amount of denial was going to change that fact. And in an act of pure cowardice, he'd invited Colin to eat with them to serve as a kind of buffer. The presence of the other man would keep Henry's impulses in check. Plus, Kellen had had hours to consider what they'd done and how ill-advised it was for him to cozy up to what was for all intents and purposes the enemy. Henry didn't think of himself as such, not even when it came to Cragmore. The duke was a wayward subject who needed to be brought to heel, not some foreign force to be subdued. Kellen was no more than a pawn in the game, and Henry had never held any bad feelings about the boy. He knew, however, that Kellen didn't see it that way — or, at least, he hadn't. Maybe... Nope, no sense in speculation. He would find out in a moment.

As soon as they entered the tent, the scent of hot soup caught his attention. Cook was waging the war against the weather in her own way, and it was much appreciated. Henry started stripping off his wet gloves as his gaze roamed around, looking for Kellen. The boy was exactly where he expected him to be, sitting by the brazier, a blanket wrapped around him for warmth. Kellen only glanced at him before his gaze skittered away.

Disappointed by the greeting and disgusted with his own expectations, he barked at Frederic. "Find Lord Kellen warmer clothes." So saying, he tossed his cloak and his gloves at his squire before heading for the decanter of wine and pouring himself a generous glass of it. He sat heavily at the table. "Help yourself, Sir Colin. I'm not going to wait on you."

"And here I was thinking you would," Colin drawled before helping himself to both the wine and the soup.

Henry didn't dare look again at Kellen, afraid his sour disposition would spill out and make the boy think he was mad at him. It didn't matter anyway, because Kellen joined them at the table, leaving his blanket behind.

He filled a glass of wine for Kellen before breaking off a piece of bread and handing it to him. "Today is the kind that requires wine before dinner. It will warm your blood, and you should fetch your blanket to help keep you from getting cold."

"That's all right," Kellen sniffed, then took a sip. "I expect the proximity to your hot temper will keep me warm."

Colin snorted.

Henry quelled the man with a hard look. "I apologize. The morning was beastly and has put me in a foul mood."

"I understand, just don't use me as an excuse to snap at your squire, if you please." Kellen's tone was as icy as the sleet and his expression distant.

Henry couldn't tell if the boy was mad at his recent conduct or regretting what they'd shared in the morning. With Colin there, it was impossible to ask. That's what he'd wanted, of course, someone to keep his tongue in check. So instead of ordering his friend to leave immediately the way he impulsively wanted to do, he hunkered down and ate his meal in silence.

Frederic returned around the time they finished eating. He held up a wool shirt and a gambeson of fine cotton for Kellen's inspection. Both were far too big for Kellen's short and slender torso. "This was all that I could find within the camp, my lord. They'll keep you warm, at least, and I can buy something that fits better in the village when the weather clears."

Henry snatched the garments before Kellen could take them. He inspected the cloth for roughness and infestation. Finding them acceptable, he handed them over to Kellen. "These seem fine. And *I'll* take you into the village as soon as the weather and my schedule permit." The possessiveness in his tone made him wince inwardly, given the audience they had. Then again, there were no two people in the entire camp that he trusted more than Colin and Frederic. They wouldn't judge him, nor would they spread tales to others.

"Thank you." Kellen directed his appreciation to the squire, not Henry, and went over to the bed to change.

Henry tracked Colin's gaze that had wandered in Kellen's direction. "Get out, Colin. Find something useful to do. You, too," he added to Frederic in a gentler tone.

Both men left without a word, leaving Henry alone with his guest, which was what he'd wanted and now regretted. He had no idea what to say to the boy, and giving into his desire to take him into his arms was definitely a bad idea.

"I don't know how to act, either." Kellen spoke in a soft tone. He'd put on both the shirt and the gambeson and was rolling up the too-long sleeves. "I've been sitting here all morning, pretending to read, and trying to make sense of how I feel."

Henry started toward the boy, who met him halfway. Neither of them reached for the other. "Do you regret what I did to you?" He held his breath waiting for an answer.

Kellen shook his head. "I can't say that I do. And yet…"

"What?"

"I don't know. Shouldn't I be ashamed…or angry or something? I barely know you, and in all likelihood, you'll kill my father and sister come springtime. I should hate you."

Henry closed the gap between them and had no trouble deciding to reach for Kellen. The boy walked into his embrace without hesitation. His head barely came up to Henry's shoulders, and now the thick layers of cloth keeping the boy warm thwarted Henry's desire to feel the contours of his body. "I will do my best to let them live. If they surrender without a fight, I'll be very happy."

"Then what?" Kellen's voice was muffled against Henry's chest.

Henry closed his eyes briefly before answering. "I send them to the king, I suppose. He's told me to quote *'use my own judgment in all matters of the siege and its aftermath'*, which means I won't know what to do until the decision is upon me. In any event, their fate is not mine to decide, as far as I'm concerned. I wish it were," he added. "I hate seeing you so upset."

"I know it's not up to you, and I don't believe that my father and sister are entitled to a second chance. True surrender is not in their nature. Oh!" Kellen pushed away from Henry and started pacing. "I don't hate you or myself for what we've done. What I hate is all of this!" He spread his arms wide. Then flopping down in his chair, he put his head between his hands. "I just want to feel at peace, at least for a little while. And being with you like…that, helped me to."

Henry's rational brain told him to only go pat the boy on the back and assure him that all would be well. He told it to shut the hell up. He went to kneel in front of Kellen. "Can I help you relax?"

Kellen eyed him with confusion. "You mean you want to kiss me again, or get back into bed so that you can..."

"No. What I have in mind doesn't involve your lips or our undressing." He used his hands to gently splay Kellen's legs and shuffled between them. "Will you let me help you?"

Kellen merely nodded.

"Good." Henry smiled. "Sit back and close your eyes."

After a moment's hesitation, Kellen complied. He jerked when Henry slid his hands up under the shirt and the gambeson to find his groin. The boy stiffened slightly as Henry plucked at the laces of his trousers, then relaxed again as Henry slowly rubbed the inside of his thigh with one hand. Kellen's eager cock greeted him as he freed it, hard and warm, ready to play.

"Please believe me, my lord, when I say that what I'm about to do pleases me as much as I hope it will relax you."

He held up the clothing with one hand while lowering his head. With his other hand, he kept Kellen's dick in place and where it needed to be for his mouth to reach it. His first touch was light, merely a lapping up and down the shaft. From the sharp intake of Kellen's breath and quivering of his body, he knew he was having the desired effect. No surprise there. He could remember his early explorations with sex and how every inch of him reacted with unbridled thrills at the least little touch. And while he'd already given Kellen his first taste of sexual pleasure that morning, there was no doubt that this was the boy's first experience at having his cock sucked. A blow job was the most intimate form of carnal pleasure as far as Henry was concerned, and one of exquisite intensity.

Young men weren't known for their self-control, especially when it came to chasing an orgasm. If he wasn't careful, it would be over before it began. So, he kept a tight grip on the base of the cock, holding any orgasm at bay. It also gave him the time he needed and wanted to savor the experience himself.

The taut skin stretched over the shaft was silky smooth and slightly salty. There was the faintest musk from their earlier efforts. Henry didn't mind. The scent of a man—natural and not perfumed like courtiers—was one of the things that excited him. He slipped his tongue through the slit on the cockhead and was rewarded with the taste of pre-cum. *Delightful.* He flicked at it a few times before swallowing the dick all the way down to the edge of his hand. He sucked and laved, happy with the moans and shivers he elicited. He could listen to the sound of Kellen's pleasure all day. But when the boy put a palm on his head and pressed, he knew it was time to stop teasing. An untried boy would only make such a move if he were desperate.

Removing his hand, Henry took the shaft farther into his mouth to its root and swallowed hard. Kellen's muted cries accompanied the strong bucking of his hips, all but levitating his ass out of the chair. It forced the dick down a fraction farther. Henry took it all and kept swallowing until he'd milked Kellen dry. He let the cock slip out of his mouth, using his tongue to swipe it clean, and sat back on his heels. He happily watched the aftershocks play across Kellen's face.

"Are you relaxed now, darling?" He didn't even question the use of the endearment. Perhaps he had no right to call the boy that on such short acquaintance, but he now thought of Lord Kellen of Cragmore as *his.*

Kellen said nothing, his chest rising and falling on hard breaths that slowly abated. The boy sprawled limply in the chair with his eyes closed. He continued to remain silent as time ticked by, and just when Henry was worried he'd somehow harmed his lover, he realized that Kellen had fallen asleep. He rose with the intent of carrying the boy to bed for a more comfortable nap. Worried that he might wake him, however, he thought better of it. Instead, he settled onto the floor beside him with his legs crossed and watched. His cock was painfully hard behind his laces. He ignored it. The thought of bringing himself to climax on his own held no appeal. If he couldn't come from Kellen's touch, he'd just have to wait. There was work for him to do, as well—probably, but he couldn't think what at the moment and didn't care. This was a siege, not a pitched battle. No one needed him more right now than Kellen did. He would watch over the boy and ponder how he would keep him safe in his arms. Whatever happened during the coming winter, it might be the only time he'd have with Kellen. He was determined to make the best of it.

Chapter Eight

"Checkmate."

Kellen's defeat came as a surprise to him, mainly because he hadn't been keeping track of the game. All his moves had been rote from experience instead of part of an effort to win. How could he possibly concentrate on the game when the man who had wrapped lips around Kellen's cock sat within touching distance? All he could think about was when would they retire for the night and what new and amazing thing were they going to do?

He sat back in his chair and toyed with his glass of wine. "You have me at a disadvantage, Baron."

Roth sat back as well and gave the kind of smile a cat might with a mouse tail hanging out of its mouth. "Do I? I can't imagine why."

Kellen tossed his head. "You know very well why. As entertaining as chess is, it's nothing compared to the other games we've played today." His cheeks warmed even as he said the words. He wasn't ever going to be able to speak casually about sex. But his embarrassment was nothing compared to his desires.

The baron drained his glass, keeping his gaze on Kellen, then stood and held out his hand. "Shall we retire, darling?"

A shiver ran up his spine. He'd heard the endearment before as he'd essentially passed out from the sheer power of his orgasm that afternoon. At least, he'd thought he was remembering correctly. Now that Roth used it again, he was certain that their relationship had shifted in a profound way. They were no longer merely captor and captive. They'd become lovers. Nothing about the situation would likely change in any essential way. The siege kept going, and they were on opposite sides of it. Still, alone here in this tent, they could shut out the world and be something else — something more and better.

Putting his unfinished glass of wine down, Kellen stood and took the proffered hand. "Please take me to bed, my lord."

Roth merely smiled as he led Kellen away from the table. "I've dismissed Frederic for the night, so we won't be disturbed." He stopped halfway to their destination and cupped Kellen's face with both his hands. "I intend to take everything slowly. I don't mean for this to be a quick tumble where I take my pleasure with no regard to you."

Kellen tipped his head up. "And why should I think otherwise? You've been nothing but kind and careful with me. I…trust you, Henry, even if we are enemies in these tedious politics." It was perhaps bold of him to use the man's given name. Like everything else, however, it felt right.

"I don't think of us that way. Your father is my enemy, whereas you are simply...*Kellen*." Henry's voice was the barest of whispers as he lowered his mouth.

The kiss started out like the first one, a light touching of the lips. It morphed quickly, though, Henry gathering him in a tight hug while sliding his mouth over Kellen's. It was astonishing to him that such a simple act could cause a massive jolt of pleasure throughout his entire body. And when Henry's tongue pressed against the seam of Kellen's lips, he experienced an even more surprising pleasure as it invaded his mouth, sweeping each corner, much the same as it had laved Kellen's dick that afternoon.

He wrapped his arms around Henry's neck, standing on tiptoes to hold him better. The height difference was challenging in a way he hadn't appreciated when they'd been lying down. Henry solved the problem by cupping Kellen's ass and lifting him. Their hard cocks mashed against each other's bodies, making them both groan. He could easily come from this muffled contact alone. As their tongues wrestled, Henry began walking again. Kellen's eyes were glued shut with passion, so he couldn't see, but their destination was obvious.

"Your pardon, my lord!" Sir Colin's voice boomed through the tent.

Henry stopped and broke off the kiss. "For God's sake, what is it, Colin?" His irritation was obvious, and hearing it helped calm Kellen's own. The baron would take care of this interruption.

The look on the knight's face was grim, nothing like his usual affable demeanor. This was no mere whim.

"There is a...situation that requires your attention. It can't wait until morning."

Henry didn't ask any further questions. He lowered Kellen to his feet. "Stay here. I'll return as soon as I can."

"Actually, Hal, Lord Kellen's presence might be helpful."

Henry frowned. "Explain yourself."

Sir Colin dropped his gaze. "An infiltrator, possibly an assassin, has been caught."

Henry swore. "Please get dressed, dar...Lord Kellen."

Kellen's stomach had tightened at the news, and with his passion replaced with rank fear, he did as he'd been asked. The weather had turned warmer again, fickle in a way that was common for the time of year, so his cotton shirt and cloak was more than enough. Within seconds, he was following Henry and Sir Colin out of the tent.

"Keep him close, Colin," Henry ordered as he strode through the camp.

Colin took Kellen by the arm and spoke low into his ear. "For your protection."

Kellen didn't like the knight's touch. There was nothing lascivious in it, but it reminded him of how his father's men thought nothing of pushing and pulling him in whatever direction they wanted, usually to his detriment. But Henry wanted this, so he forced himself to relax and not fight the grip.

The camp was quieter than usual, not completely silent because the men around them murmured to each other. The tension was easy to detect, though, and it had an ugly edge to it. Most of the soldiers had their hands on the hilt of either a sword or a knife, making it clear they expected trouble.

The source of the concern wasn't far away. A young man was being held between a young soldier and Sir Hugh, his face bloody, and he was undressed down to his rough tunic and trousers. Even his feet were bare, save for the kind of strips that the lower born used for socks. It would have been pitiable the way the boy shivered in the cold, except for the look of pure hatred on his face as Henry approached. Kellen tried to stick close to the man, but Colin held him back.

Henry stood in front of the prisoner. "What is going on?" His question was directed to the soldiers holding him, although his gaze was fixed on the boy.

"We caught this one sneaking through the camp, my lord," Sir Hugh explained. "He would have gone unnoticed but for this." The man used his free hand to rub at the boy's head.

It was then that Kellen noticed how the captive's dark hair poorly hid the white-blond beneath what had to be some kind of boot polish. And as he stared more closely, his heart sank. *I know him.*

The security chief of the camp continued. "I might not have taken any notice if he'd stuck to his natural color. Plenty of our lads are from similar places as the North. But the obvious effort to conceal it caught my attention. He has not yet said who he is or where he comes from, but he was loaded with a short sword and several knives in his belt and in his boots. We came to the obvious conclusion, Baron."

Henry nodded. "And his bruises?"

"Put up a fight, he did, my lord. Tried to get his licks in, too." Sir Hugh tugged at the collar of his cloak to show how he'd been nicked by some kind of blade.

Henry braced his legs and folded his arms. "Who are you?"

The prisoner sneered. "Fuck off."

When the young soldier opposite Sir Hugh drew back his free hand to cuff the boy, Henry stopped him with a gesture. "Are you from the Highrock?" When the captive simply glared, Henry sighed. "You aren't going to make this easy, are you? No surprise, I suppose."

Sir Hugh shook the boy by the arm he held. "We'll loosen his tongue, my lord."

"The king has been clear that we must comport ourselves as the rules of his army normally dictate when dealing with an enemy. We must not give the people of the North any reason to believe their duke's tales of the king's oppression, either. I share his feelings on both points.

"I doubt any amount of torture will work, anyway," Henry continued. "He has the look of a fanatic. I'm not sure it matters, in any event. If the intent was to assassinate me, it was a predictable move. The only thing we need to know is where he came from." He looked in the direction of Highrock, looming in the distance as always. "If he got out, we can get in. Set loose the trackers and their hounds. We'll see if they can figure out the path he took to get here."

Kellen desperately wanted to shout that he knew. He clamped his mouth shut, however. His loyalty to his family was not absolute, but he couldn't bring himself to betray them, nevertheless.

Henry turned to leave. In the next moment, there was a blur of movement and loud cries. The prisoner lunged toward Henry with a knife, sticking him in the side. Henry stumbled to his knees, even as Sir Hugh twisted the boy's arm. The knife went straight into the prisoner's stomach as the two of them wrestled. He fell to the ground, gasping a few times before becoming still.

Kellen jerked free of Colin and ran to his lover. "Henry!" He slid to his knees and grabbed the man by his shoulders. "How bad is it? Let me see."

Henry looked at him and spoke through clenched teeth. "Hurts like a bitch. It's nothing," he added as he clutched his now-red hands to the wound.

Colin joined them. "Let go a minute, Hal." He pried Henry's hands away and studied where the blood seeped from. "I'll help you to your tent. Somebody fetch the doctor!" The knight glared at the soldier who had lost his knife to the prisoner, then shifted his gaze to Sir Hugh. "And you have a little *chat* with that one about the proper way to search and guard a prisoner. In the meantime, get rid of that." He jerked his chin toward the dead boy.

"Aye, sir." With obvious fury, Sir Hugh gestured to some nearby soldiers. "You know what to do, lads. Come on," he said to the hapless soldier. "Let's review your training." He grabbed the boy by the arm much as he'd done with the prisoner and pulled him away.

Not wanting to leave his lover's side, Kellen refused to heed Sir Colin's silent order to get back. Instead, he helped Henry to his feet and didn't let go, even as the man stood steady. He walked slowly but strongly back to his tent with his head held high. Now as they passed the throng of men, there was total silence. Everyone bowed their head in an obvious show of respect. When their heads came up again, however, Kellen saw the hatred in their eyes. What had been merely bored men were now soldiers out for blood. Kellen tried not to cower at those looks. It was hard because he understood that if they broke loose from Henry's control, the first person to die would be Kellen.

He put aside his fears and focused on the more urgent matter of helping his wounded lover. Between the two of them, Sir Colin and Kellen undressed Henry and laid him out on the bed. The baron said nothing, but the set of his jaw and harsh breathing spoke of the pain he was in. The knight replaced Henry's hands with a clean towel, and in that brief moment of exchange, Kellen was relieved to see that the cut appeared shallow.

The doctor arrived, forcing Kellen to step away and hover around the periphery as the skinny, older man did his work. He loomed his thin frame over Henry, his long, sharp nose practically pressed against the site of the wound.

"Hmm, not bad. Not bad at all, my lord." The doctor stood, his bony shoulders in a shrug. "You were lucky."

"I would have been luckier if the night had been colder and I had worn my gambeson, Doctor Allen." Henry's voice was strong, even as his pain was obvious. He looked in Kellen's direction. "I'm fine. Please don't worry."

If the doctor thought it strange that the baron was reassuring his other, still-living prisoner, he didn't show it. He went about his business, pouring some concoction down Henry's throat before cleaning the wound with a bowl of warm water that Frederic had brought in, then sowing the ragged edges shut and binding a thick wad of cloth against it.

"As I said, my lord…lucky. You should be back to your usual self in a few days. I'll come back in the morning to change the dressing." Then he did something extraordinary by handing a bottle over to Kellen. "See that he takes a spoonful of this twice during the night. It will ease his pain and ward off putridness. It's an amazing concoction newly acquired from Shadow Valley. Quite remarkable, really, and I've added my own pain remedy to it."

Kellen took the medicine with gratitude. "Thank you, sir. I'll make sure he takes it."

The older man nodded, packed up his bag, and added, "And no strenuous activities for the foreseeable future." He looked down his long nose meaningfully.

Kellen felt his face heat. "Yes, sir."

Doctor Allen left with a spritely gate that belied his age.

Kellen, Sir Colin and Frederic stood staring at each other for a few seconds before Henry spoke. "I thank you all for your help, but it's time for you to leave, Colin and Frederic. I'll be fine with Lord Kellen to play nursemaid." His speech was tired-sounding, an effect of the medicine, no doubt, as well as the energy it must have taken to walk back as if nothing were wrong with him.

Sir Colin didn't hesitate to obey. "I'll see what progress the trackers have made and report to you in the morning." He paused at the tent flap. "You really are lucky, Hal. And that soldier's lack of vigilance just emphasizes that we are commanding men that we haven't personally trained. This siege has to break sooner rather than later." He gave Kellen a hard look before leaving.

Frederic stood wringing his hands. "Are you sure, my lord? Tending to you is my duty."

Henry managed an indulgent smile. "And you do it admirably so, Frederic. Not tonight, though. Go seek your bed."

Frederic, too, stared at Kellen. The boy was frowning, then his expression suddenly morphed into one of acceptance. "Yes, my lord. I dare say Lord Kellen can be trusted with your care." With that, he left.

Kellen rushed to Henry's bedside. He put the medicine bottle on the table and picked up the wet cloth. "Let me clean your hands." Not daring to look at his lover in the face, he began scrubbing away the dried blood from when Henry had pressed against his wound.

"I don't blame you," Henry said quietly. He lifted his first clean hand to cup Kellen's cheek. "My feelings for you are the same as they were before we were so rudely interrupted."

Kellen paused in his efforts. "And what are they...your feelings?" He held his breath waiting for the answer.

"I'm not sure." Henry's arm dropped heavily to the mattress, testament to how weak he was, despite the stabbing being shallow.

Kellen submerged the towel into the water, which had grown cold, and took the bowl over to the dining table. "It doesn't matter." He kept his face turned away, lest his lover see his disappointment. *What did I expect, a declaration of his undying love?* "You must rest now." He eyed his usual seat by the brazier. That was where he'd have to sleep this night.

"Darling, come here." Even in a soft tone, Henry's words were commanding.

Kellen went back to him, his heart partially mollified by the endearment, although he tried not to get his hopes up. He stood by the side of the bed once more. "Don't tax yourself. We can...talk later."

"We will talk now." With obvious effort, Henry slid closer to the middle of the bed. "Lie down here with me."

Kellen shook his head, even as he desperately wanted to obey. "I'll cause you pain and disturb your sleep."

Henry merely gave him a stern look and patted the mattress. When Kellen started to comply, the man stopped him with, "Oh, and take off your clothes."

Kellen rolled his eyes at the notion that a man stabbed only a short while ago would be interested in satisfying his dick. Nevertheless, he complied, shivering slightly once he was completely naked. He slid into bed, pulling the covers up to keep them both warm.

He lay on his back and stared up at the ceiling of the tent. "Now will you go to sleep?"

"It's too early. I'm weak from my injury, but not tired as such." He paused. "I like you, Kellen, and it's not about the sex. That's amazing, to be sure, but my desire for you is more than that. I like spending time with you, playing chess, eating or simply sitting and reading. It's quite extraordinary. I've never felt this way with another man before.

"Oh, I like spending time with Colin, even though he isn't much of a reader and makes for a poor opponent in chess. And yes, we've pleasured each other often as a release only. We've never slept in the same bed, let alone wrapped around each other. You are different, Kellen."

Warmed by the confession, Kellen rolled onto his side facing Henry. "I feel the same way. And it's not only about the sex with me, either." As he pondered what more he could say, he noticed that Henry's cock was tenting the covers. "How can you be aroused after what you've been through?"

Henry turned his head to look at him. "I have a beautiful, naked boy lying beside me. How could I not be hard?"

Kellen flopped onto his back once again and blew out a breath. "I don't understand men, even though I am one. We can't have sex. It would aggravate your wound, and climaxing can't be good for you."

Henry chuckled. "I disagree. Orgasms are always good for one's health, and we can have a form of sex, if you're willing to do all the work."

Kellen was intrigued. He couldn't help himself. "What do you mean?"

Henry exposed them both by shoving down the covers as far as his arm could reach. Two dicks bobbed with freedom, because Kellen couldn't help being aroused, either.

"Straddle my legs. Right above the knees," Henry clarified before Kellen could object. "That's it," the man encouraged when Kellen moved to do as he suggested.

He hovered over his lover, not daring to put his weight on any part of him. "Now what?"

"Now you sit." Henry grabbed hold of Kellen's waist with one hand and pushed him down.

Kellen positioned his feet so that he could sit on his heels instead of putting his full weight on Henry. Their cocks brushed. He couldn't keep the gasp from flying out of his mouth.

Henry slid his fingers up Kellen's shaft before letting his arm drop again. "I want you to do to us the same as I did in bed this morning. Remember?"

"How could I forget my first experience with sex?" The memory of it caused his cock to jerk and his balls to tighten.

"I shall never forget myself, but as much as I want to do it again, I don't have the strength. The doctor's concoction has dulled me, and as you said, getting stabbed was a shock to my body. Will you do the work, darling? Please?"

There was no way to refuse, especially as Kellen wanted this contact more than he could say. His guilt over possibly hurting his lover failed to override their desires. With only a slight hesitation, he clasped the shafts with one hand. He knew immediately that it wouldn't work. He couldn't wrap his fingers around enough of both dicks to jerk them properly. Instead, he took his own with one hand and Henry's with his other. He still had trouble holding onto much of the man's shaft. There was no help for it, so he concentrated on playing with his lover's cockhead, stimulating the bundle of nerves underneath it. He'd learned by pleasuring himself that this was a sensitive part of a dick. And at the same time, he jerked the shaft as best he could.

Kellen mirrored the movements he made to himself, finding a rhythm and increasing his efforts once he established it. Henry lay with his eyes closed and his fingers clenched around the bedding. The way his muscled abdomen rippled with each stroke and his breath hitched, Kellen knew he was getting it at least partially right. His own pleasure grew until he couldn't keep his eyes open. An orgasm ripped through him, throwing his movements out of sync. It hardly mattered because Henry was right there with him, his cum spurting out to splash Kellen's hand.

When they were both finished, he reluctantly let go, slid off Henry and washed each of them with a clean towel. He turned down the lamps, then he climbed back into bed, wanting to talk, but not saying anything. Henry's steady breathing told him that he'd done the man some good after all. Closing his eyes, he drifted off, too.

* * * *

Kellen woke abruptly from a deep sleep from the bed rocking. He opened his eyes to see a large body leaning across his. "Henry, what are you doing?"

"Sorry, darling. I didn't mean to wake you."

Henry pulled back to his side of the bed. "I need this medicine to help with the pain. Shallow it may be, this wound still hurts." He unstopped the flask and drank deeply."

Kellen sat up and tugged the medicine from his lover's hand. "The doctor said to take a teaspoon, not glug it down like ale." He set the bottle back on the table and glared at the man.

"Don't worry, darling. I didn't drink too much." He put his hand on Kellen's knee. "How are you feeling?"

Kellen frowned. "Why do you ask? I wasn't the one who was stabbed."

Henry rubbed his thumb along the outside of Kellen's calf. "I didn't mean physically. You knew that boy, didn't you?"

Kellen's heart sank, not because he wasn't prepared to admit everything to Henry, but because it was sooner than he'd expected. "I didn't know him so much as recognized him."

"He was from the castle." It wasn't a question.

Kellen couldn't look at him as he answered. While the tent was gloomy this far from sunrise, the banked brazier and the hole in the ceiling for the smoke to go through gave off enough light for them to see. "His name was Garth, and he was one of the pages...and my sister's bed toy."

"Toy?"

"You know, someone she commanded into her bed purely for pleasure. Isolde isn't one to form friendships, let alone fall in love. I don't think I ever saw her talk to him except to order him about. I bet he saw their relationship differently. He did this for her."

"I see." Henry squeezed Kellen's knee. "Look at me. Please."

Kellen turned to do so.

"There is a way in and out of the castle other than the obvious one, isn't there?"

Kellen was ashamed to admit it yet also ashamed to deny it. "Yes." He couldn't keep the anguish from his tone, nor stop the tears that leaked out.

"Oh, darling, come lie beside me."

Kellen gratefully complied. At least his confession wasn't angering Henry. The man had suspected he knew more than he told, but apparently the confirmation didn't upset him enough to cast Kellen aside.

He wiped his face with impatience. "I couldn't tell you before."

"I understand." Henry's voice was low and soothing. "Please don't cry. Your tears hurt me more than the knife did."

Kellen scrubbed his face more, but the crying didn't abate no matter his efforts. "I should tell you where to find the way in. I just don't want to be a traitor. No matter what, I am a Cragmore. How can I go against my own people?"

His body began to shake as his crying turned into sobbing. He kept as quiet as he could, mindful that more and extra-vigilant guards were right outside the tent. His anguish was for Henry only.

Henry did his best to soothe him with hushed tones. He tried to tug Kellen closer to his side. Kellen rebuffed him, knowing that it was only because of Henry's weakened state that he was able to. As much as he longed for the man's comfort, he wasn't going to aggravate the wound. He was already causing the man pain with his stubborn confusion of what he owed his lover compared to his family. Regardless, Henry held his hand throughout.

When he was finally able to get himself back under control, Henry squeezed his hand.

"I understand, Kellen, that being a Cragmore means being loyal to your family." He paused as if marshaling his thoughts. "What if you were a Roth? Would being loyal to your new family make a difference?"

Kellen's breath caught. He stuttered it out with difficulty before speaking. "What are you asking?"

"I'm asking you to marry me, darling. Become my baroness, and help me end this siege."

It was foolish of him to feel disappointed that he was being courted as a means to an end. Still, his heart ached. Against all reason, he understood at that moment he'd fallen in love with Henry. Marrying him would be the fulfillment of a fantasy he hadn't known he possessed. Here it was being realized, though, except it wasn't born out of Henry feeling the same way.

His dismay was not something he could push aside. "I'm a useful tool, then. Bind me to you simply to find the secret entrance. And after the siege ends? What will you do? You'd be tied to someone you don't want."

Henry had the audacity to chuckle. "I'm sorry, darling. I know this is a difficult moment for you, but please be assured that I want you…very much so. I wouldn't offer this as a solution to any other Cragmore."

Somewhat mollified and knowing he was being silly, Kellen gave the only acceptable answer. "I'll consider it. I never thought to marry for love, and if it saves many lives, my wants don't count, anyway."

Henry squeezed his hand again. "You're wrong about that. You and what you desire count very much. When this siege is over, I'll show you how true my words are."

Suddenly exhausted from it all, Kellen shut his eyes. "Go to sleep, my lord. You'll have my answer in the morning." That was a lie because Kellen already knew what he'd do. There was really no choice, and his heart would have to get used to having the man he loved, even though he didn't love him back. It was better than not having Henry at all—or so he told himself.

Chapter Nine

Henry paced around his tent, ignoring the hitch at his side. Two days of bed rest was plenty. His wound was clean and sufficiently trivial that he wasn't going to give it any more consideration. As he made his laps, he tried not to stare at Kellen, who was sitting quietly in his chair by the brazier. The boy had accepted his proposal the morning after the attack with the same amount of enthusiasm as Henry had shown his childhood tutors — with practical resignation. Although Kellen didn't say as much, Henry knew that his acquiescence was done out of duty and not affection.

"I never thought to marry for love..."

Those words had cut deeper than the would-be assassin's knife. He couldn't say why, exactly. He could have said the same thing because he hadn't expected to marry, either. With Prince Soren's as the prime example, Moorcondia was becoming quite sanguine about men marrying each other. And he knew for a fact that his cousin had recently married her childhood playmate, proving that women could marry each other just as well. Taking Kellen as his baroness wasn't anything remarkable, and it was an important solution to breaking the siege. What difference did it make if Kellen loved him. *Do I even love* him? The fact that he dared ask himself the question was startling.

He stopped his wanderings in front of Kellen. "Are you all right, darling?"

The boy stared back at him, his expression unreadable. "After the ceremony this morning, do you expect me to show you the way into the castle immediately?"

Henry knew what the answer should be. With each passing day, his men became more restless. The assassin had stoked a simmering fire, and while Henry had a firm grip on his men, he also knew that most of them had never served under him. The king had ordered a wide group of fighting brigades for this effort. With the Marshers and the Swarm subdued, soldiers could be drawn away from other fronts. He couldn't count on preventing many of them from slipping their leash, no matter what he did. Once the dam broke, the villagers would be at risk as easy targets for the men's wrath. He didn't dare contemplate having to order his men to fight each other to quell the ranks. Time was something they had little of.

"No," he said instead. "We'll have a proper wedding night first."

That answer seemed to brighten Kellen's mood. Before the boy could respond, however, Colin came in, his face extra grim.

Henry became alarmed. "What is it?"

"Father Paul has respectfully declined to officiate the wedding."

That was not what Henry had expected and oddly, it infuriated him more than any rebellion would have. "The fuck he has!"

Colin shrugged. "He doesn't hold with—and I quote—*'this new abomination of the marriage sacrament'* and has voiced his views to the king personally."

"Seriously? Gods, what kind of idiot insults the king's family?" Henry rubbed the back of his neck. "Well, that explains why he was sent on this mission to freeze his balls off. Is there no one else?"

Colin nodded his head toward Kellen. "What do you think, my lord? Would Reverend Mother Therese be willing to marry you and the baron?"

"Oh." Kellen stood. "I think she would. She's a practical woman, and if this helps end the siege with as little bloodshed as possible, she'll be supportive. We can but ask."

That settled matters. "Then we go. Colin, our horses, if you please. And I want you to stay here," he added before his bannerman got any ideas of coming with them. "I need someone trustworthy and wielding a strong hand to keep this camp under control."

"Yes, my lord."

As Colin left, Henry held out his hand to Kellen. "Let us get married, darling."

* * * *

It was a nice day for a celebration of any kind. As Henry trotted up the winding road to the abbey, he couldn't help but admire the bright sun and the crisp air. The wind was low and the temperature still sufficiently mild that a simple shirt and cloak were all that was needed for warmth. *There will be less for me to disrobe from Kellen*. Ah yes, that was the bonus of this idea to marry the boy. Making him a Roth and thereby shifting his allegiance was an important goal, but bedding the boy was definitely an excellent side benefit.

Seeing Kellen astride his horse, his cloak wrapped around his slight body, hair neatly braided down his back, Henry couldn't help wanting him. He already knew what lay beneath the clothing and Kellen had proved to be an eager bedmate. Henry could only hope that the forced marriage — as that was what it was — wouldn't dampen the boy's ardor. And even if it did, Henry intended to try to end the siege without killing the duke and his daughter. Hopefully, Kellen would be able in time to lose his anger and accept their life together, because Henry was determined that they would have one. Picturing Kellen by his side for the rest of his life didn't worry him. To the contrary, it made him content in a surprising way. It might be the stirrings of love. He couldn't say, having never known it before. But if it were only friendship, that would have to suffice.

Kellen turned his head toward him. "What? Why are you staring at me?"

"Sorry. It's simply that you are lovely to look at."

"Huh!" With a toss of his head, Kellen returned his attention to the road ahead of him. The sudden stain of pink on his cheeks told Henry that the boy wasn't unaffected by the compliment.

The time for ogling and talking came to an abrupt end as they rounded a curve and arrived at a tall stone wall with an iron gate across the road. Henry held up his hand to stop their entourage. There were a couple of dozen reliable soldiers with them, more than would have been necessary if an assassin hadn't managed to sneak into the camp. The large number of soldiers was intended to act as a deterrent. The misguided boy might not be the only one with the same idea of getting rid of Henry, and while he wasn't worried about his ability to defend himself, he didn't want Kellen caught in the middle of a fight.

Henry swung out of his saddle to approach the gate, not surprised when Kellen came alongside him. There was a large bell set into the wall. Henry gave it a few tugs, making a loud pealing sound. When he saw no one approaching from the abbey, he reached to do it again.

Kellen stayed his hand. "This time of day, they'll be at prayer. Give them some time. I assure you they heard the bell."

As the boy knew this convent better than he did, Henry took his advice and waited as patiently as a soldier could. He wanted to spend the time kissing his wife-to-be. His men would understand, but Kellen would be embarrassed, he was sure. He'd caused the boy enough distress, so he clasped his hands to keep them to himself and watched for the sight of an approaching nun.

When women did come, three of them with their habits billowing out behind them, he was surprised to see the reverend mother, herself. It had to be her, given that she wore the higher wimple that was the sign of her elevated station.

The older woman stopped by the gates and spread her arms wide. "Lord Kellen, we are grateful to the gods for bringing you back to us."

Kellen stepped closer to the bars. "And I am glad to see you again, Reverend Mother. I'm well, as you can see, and Baron Roth and I have come to ask a favor of you."

The woman regarded Henry with a shrewd and distrusting gaze. "What could he need from us? It can't be more wine. I'm sure someone as important as the baron doesn't lower himself to do the shopping."

Kellen actually smiled at that, then surprised Henry by holding out his hand. "No, ma'am. The baron and I would like you to marry us."

Taking the proffered hand, Henry bowed to the woman. "Reverend Mother, would you please do us the honor?"

The woman tucked her hands into her wide sleeves, not even trying to hide her surprise. "This is a strange turn of events, to be sure. This is what you want, Lord Kellen?"

"Yes." The fact that the boy didn't hesitate to answer relieved Henry's concern. "Our union will join our houses and help end the siege. It's the best path forward, Reverend Mother."

"I see. Is there no servant of the gods available at the siege camp to perform this ceremony?" Her question made clear her worry that there was an ulterior motive for Henry to gain access to the abbey.

"Yes," Kellen replied. "But he won't marry two men because he doesn't believe in such a union."

The reverend mother lifted her face to the sky. "Gods save us from the self-righteous. Of course I shall perform the rite." She nodded to the nuns on either side of her, and the women pulled the ropes to open the gates. "Only you and the baron may enter. The others will wait out here." Her tone brooked no disagreement.

Henry was happy to oblige. There was probably no safer place for him and Kellen than the abbey. He turned to his most senior soldier, a solid man who could be counted on not to do anything foolish. "Make camp here. We'll be back before nightfall."

"You will see them in the morning," the reverend mother corrected.

Surprised and delighted to find that he would have the chance for privacy with his wife on their wedding night, he happily repeated the statement before entering into the secret world of women.

Henry didn't bother to hide his curiosity. This was the place where Kellen had chosen to spend most of his time. He wanted to see for himself what attracted the boy to the abbey in general and winemaking in particular. With winter nearly upon them, the vineyard off in the distance was hauntingly beautiful in its own way. And it appeared to be in poor shape.

"Are they dead?" he asked, waving in the direction of the vineyard.

Kellen choked off a laugh. "No, the vines are merely dormant. There's a lot going on underground, and when spring arrives, they will come to life again. Perhaps I'll have time to give you a quick tour of the winery — if you're interested, that is."

Henry gazed at his wife-to-be. "I'm interested in anything that has to do with you. We have a small wine production at Rothberg, my family seat. It's not nearly as large as the sisters' appears to be, but I hope you will find it of interest to manage."

Kellen's eyes widened with obvious interest. "I would love that." Then he banked his enthusiasm. "Although it must be well-run already, and I don't want to intrude on someone else's domain."

Henry brought him to a stop, because it was important for the boy to understand. "Rothberg is mine, and as my wife, you will have great power there. Whatever you want to do, you will do, and no one would even think of gainsaying you. It's your proper role to run the property with me."

A throat-clearing by the reverend mother had him walking again, trudging up a stone path to the top of a not-insubstantial hill where the abbey sat. In its own way, the place was nearly as siege-proof as Highrock. If only Kellen had stayed put, he would never have been found and remained as safe as possible from the conflict. *But then he wouldn't be mine.* The fierce possessiveness that caught him by the throat was nearly alarming. He felt almost out of control now in his quest to marry the boy. It was important for him to keep his emotions in check. The night to come had to be done right, and by that, it meant going slowly. His cock would have to accept that it couldn't have what it wanted right away.

The marriage, by contrast, was nearly upon them. As they entered the abbey, the temperature dropped noticeably. He was glad that he'd insisted that Kellen dress in all the layers of clothing he had. When the siege was over, he would take the boy shopping for a full array of everything he needed and befitted a baroness, albeit a male one. They followed the reverend mother down a long hall. At the end of it, massive wooden doors stood open, and beyond those was a beautiful chapel with gleaming wooden pews and long, tapered candles that bathed the place in a soft, almost-romantic, light. The reverend mother went to the sanctuary and picked up a large leather-bound book. She placed it on a podium and waited for them to join her.

She looked down her nose at them, but not unkindly. "Marriage is a solemn occasion. It's not something I have many chances to participate in, and I'm honored to do it. Words must be spoken and vows made. It is for life. Do each of you come here of your own volition, fully intending to be bound to each other?"

Henry let Kellen answer first, knowing that the warning was for the boy's benefit more than his.

"Yes, I do." There was no hesitation in Kellen's response, his voice being steady and loud.

"As do I," Henry agreed, more relieved than he would have admitted that Kellen hadn't balked at the last moment.

"Then we shall begin." The woman opened her book and began the ceremony in the time-honored tradition of Moorcondia. Cragmore might be in rebellion to form his own country, but the North still practiced the customs of their country. This union would be binding anywhere they went.

Henry let out a breath that he hadn't realized he'd been holding and soon, sooner than he would have expected, he had a wife.

* * * *

Kellen gestured around them with one of his hands. "I've participated in all the stages of making the wine."

Henry walked along, taking everything in and content to be the follower for once instead of the leader.

Even with the sun setting early, they had time to tour the abbey's winery. As he explained everything, Kellen spoke in an animated voice. His passion for what he did was obvious. It made Henry even more determined to give his wife free rein at the Rothberg vineyards. *My wife.* The words were foreign to him, yet also filled his heart with an unnameable feeling. *Coward. I know what I feel.* Affection was too pale a word for what was growing inside him. Love might be too strong in their new relationship—but only a little bit. He was smitten, as his grandmother would have said. And that was as good a word as any to use. Kellen hadn't released his hand from Henry's, and he found he liked the contact—not passionate, yet pleasurable in its own way.

They stopped by a large copper vat with a fire pit beneath it. "Here's where the grapes go after they've been squeezed."

"And how does that happen exactly, the pulping part?"

Kellen grinned. "The nuns stomp on them in wide barrels with their bare feet."

Henry reared back. "You are making that up, surely?"

Now his wife laughed. "No, I'm not. That's how it's done. I swear. You don't think I'd lie to my husband, do you?"

Henry tugged the boy closer and took him in his arms. "I like hearing that word—'husband', and I like saying the word 'wife'."

Kellen dipped his gaze. "You haven't said it yet."

"No? I must rectify that error right now. Wife." He said the word with reverence before leaning down to take Kellen's mouth in a kiss.

It was supposed to be light, respectful both to the fact that Kellen was now his wife and mindful of where they were. That proved impossible. A taste was never going to be enough. He needed more. With his hand holding Kellen's head in place, he devoured the boy's mouth, invading it with his tongue and swallowing his breathy moans. They were both hard, and just as Henry thought he might dare to find a secluded corner to do more, a great bell pealed.

Kellen broke away. "That's announcing supper."

Henry let go reluctantly. "Damn."

Kellen's eyes flashed. "Don't worry. Men aren't allowed in the nuns' private area. We'll spend the night in the little cell I use off the great hall. Someone will have provided food for us. We'll be all alone."

Grabbing his wife's hand, Henry raced out of the winery. He wouldn't waste another moment. His need to get Kellen on a pallet in seclusion made his feet fly. Better still, Kellen kept up with him. Eventually, he had to yield to his wife to show him where to go. Kellen brought him to a small cell off the entryway that housed male guests. The nuns didn't trust men in their private space, and he could hardly blame them.

The chamber wasn't much—a pallet piled high with comforters to make up for the lack of a brazier, a small table and a couple of chairs. Someone had left two plates filled with a chicken casserole, fresh bread, a jug of water and…a bottle of wine.

Kellen cried out in delight as he lifted the wine. "This is my favorite and a good pairing with a hearty chicken dish." He poured them both a glass and held one out to Henry. "To us and our new marriage."

Henry had no trouble toasting to that. As he took a healthy swallow of the wine, he found he liked it, too. And he spotted a small bottle on the other side of the water jug. It obviously contained oil, and he nearly blushed himself at the realization that some nun knew enough about the workings of men's bodies to provide a lubricant. He'd brought some cream but had not thought to snatch it from his saddlebag once he learned they'd be spending the night in the abbey. He'd been concerned that he'd have to make do with spit, and that was far from optimal. Tonight would be Kellen's first time being breached, and it was critical that it be as enjoyable as it could be.

He pulled out one of the chairs for his wife. "Shall we eat, darling?"

Kellen sat. "Yes, please. I'm starving." Picking up his fork, he shoveled some casserole in his mouth. "Sister Johanna is an excellent cook. And she always makes sure I have a lot of food." He eyed the piece of bread Henry had broken off and was offering him. "I best eat less than I normally should, don't you think? I don't want to be...too full for tonight when we retire."

Henry pressed the bread into his hand. "I'll make sure we wait a sufficient amount of time after supper before we do so."

Kellen nodded and bit off a piece of bread.

Henry started in on his own meal, agreeing completely about the good sister's skills. He'd rarely tasted better, and simple food though it might be, it was still delicious. It chased the chill from him, as did the wine. He eyed the pallet to judge how well they'd stay warm throughout the night. The nuns had to shiver through the winter in these cold cells.

"We aren't going to be able to fully undress if we want to keep out the cold. There's only so much my talents can do to keep your blood heated."

Kellen choked and washed his mouthful down with wine. "The things you say, Henry. Or should I call you Hal? Sir Colin does."

"Hal's a childhood nickname. Few people use it now, but you are welcome to."

"I like Henry better. It's a noble and powerful name, so it suits you."

Pleased by the compliment, Henry tried not to preen. "You'll give me a big head, wife."

"I only speak the truth. I promise I'll never say anything that isn't true simply to appease you. I'm done with living that way." Gesturing to the pallet, he added, "There are bedwarmers under the covers, which from experience I can tell you are thick and excellent in keeping out the cold. Besides, you're like a human-sized brazier, don't you know?"

Now it was Henry's turn to choke as his swallow morphed into a chuckle. "I appreciate your honesty, but no one has ever said as much before, wife."

Kellen stared at him with bright eyes. "I think you like saying that word, don't you? Wife? There's a look in your eyes and a tone that you're using I've never heard before." He shrugged and looked away. "Maybe it's my imagination."

Leaning toward the boy, Henry brushed his lips over Kellen's. "I do like it, as it happens. Let's hurry up and finish our meal so that I can start to show you how much."

Chapter Ten

Kellen clasped his hands to stop the tiny trembles that had snuck up on him as he'd sat down from where Henry — *my husband* — had cleared the bedwarmers off the pallet. The covers were toasty warm, but that was nothing compared to the heat in Henry's eyes that warmed Kellen right to his core and made him hard and aching. His hole clenched, as well, although part of that was from fear. He'd seen Henry's cock, and he knew how small his own hole was. It seemed impossible that the two would fit together, yet men did it all the time, and no one seemed the worse for it.

Stop fretting. Henry knows what to do.

He wasn't fooling the man, either. Henry knelt in front of him to tug off Kellen's boots as he'd done his own already. Then he pulled Kellen's hands apart and held them. "Please don't be afraid."

"I'm not." Kellen knew his denial wasn't very convincing.

"Nervous, then." Henry lifted each hand in turn and kissed the backs of them. "I won't do anything to hurt you, darling, and we'll take this as slow as needed. We have all night, and I won't enjoy any moment of it if you aren't."

Kellen blew out a breath. "I already know your touch gives me the greatest pleasure I've ever known." He had to look away. "It's just that *one* thing. You know?"

"I understand. And I can't promise that it won't be uncomfortable, because it always is the first time. It can't be helped, but I'll make sure you are as ready as possible before I mount you."

Just hearing the words sent a shiver down Kellen's spine. "I want it, you know. I've dreamed about it. I won't disappoint you," he added, because he worried that a virile man like Henry would grow tired of a delicate virgin.

"Of course you won't, darling, because that would be impossible. Being with you is a great joy, and knowing that I have you all to myself is enough to make my dick hard and my balls ache." He ran fingers lightly down Kellen's cheek. "You are the most beautiful creature I have ever seen. How did I get to be so lucky?"

Kellen turned his face to nuzzle his husband's palm. "I'm the lucky one, Henry. My life has been empty without you, full of nastiness. I never expected to be happy, only being content with making wine with the sisters. If I'd been born a girl, I would have taken my vows simply to escape to this peaceful place. Now…" He shook his head, unable to put his feelings into the right words anymore.

"Selfishly, I'm glad you weren't. And your life will be filled with as much happiness as I can give you." Henry used his finger to raise Kellen's chin before kissing him. As always, the kiss started out soft and gentle. It quickly changed to hungry and demanding, Henry pressing Kellen onto his back as he devoured his mouth.

The man roamed his hands seemingly everywhere on Kellen's body, even as he thrust his tongue inside Kellen's mouth. Every touch made him shudder and moan. He grabbed as much of his husband as he could reach and tried to give as good as he was getting, avoiding the bandage that still wrapped around his husband's middle. Henry acted as if he were fully mended. Kellen knew better. A wound like that would take time to heal. He needed to be as careful with his husband as the man was being with him.

Their hard cocks rubbed against each other, but the layers of clothing were frustrating. He wanted to feel all of Henry.

He broke the kiss to make his wishes known. "Strip me, Henry. I want you to be able to touch all of me, skin-to-skin."

Henry nuzzled Kellen's neck. "I don't want you to get chilled, darling."

"Impossible with you draped over me like a blanket."

His husband didn't argue with him, instead removing first Kellen's shirt, then his trousers and small clothes. The way the cotton rasped against his aroused dick nearly made him come. Henry quickly grabbed it at the root once he'd tossed the clothing on the floor.

Kellen arched into the frustration of not finding his release. "Why do you do that?"

Henry chuckled against throat as he lapped his way down. "It's to stop you from coming, darling. The frustration makes the climax that much more intense."

Kellen clenched at his shoulders and shuddered some more. "I-If you say so." He had to trust that when it came to sex, Henry knew what he was doing — except the man still had his clothes on.

Kellen tugged at Henry's shirt, trying to pull it over his head. "I want to touch you, too. All of you."

Henry somehow managed to help to strip himself while still holding onto Kellen's cock and without breaking the lavish attention his lips and tongue were giving Kellen's body, from neck to pecs and on to nipples. He sucked one nub in and worked it with his tongue. With the orgasm being choked, it was exquisite torture.

Kellen writhed, and with Henry's skin now available, he couldn't help but dig his nails into it. "Please, Henry."

Henry lipped down Kellen's belly. "Please, what?"

"Let me come. You're being mean, husband."

"Oh, you think so. Well, let me show you how generous I can be."

Kellen didn't understand what the man meant until he replaced his hand with his mouth. In one motion, he had sucked the shaft nearly to the root. This was familiar territory, and Kellen knew that it wouldn't take much of this kind of attention to make him come quickly. But there was more. He'd nearly missed how his husband had shifted both their bodies so that Henry could slip his hand between Kellen's legs. A finger circled his hole. It was a gentle touch made slick by something.

The oil. He'd rather hoped it was just there as a seasoning for the bread and maybe that was what had been intended. Henry was simply putting it to better use, regardless of what the sister who'd brought their supper had expected. He just couldn't bear the idea that nuns understood the ins and outs of anal sex.

The sucking of his cock, as well as the smallness of the finger, made it easy for him to relax and take it when Henry slipped it past the ring. Once that happened, he became mindless with pleasure. There was something inside him that connected to his dick, because when Henry pressed the pad of his finger against it, Kellen came with blinding force. He bit his lower lip to keep from crying out. Their cell was secluded, but he wasn't used to being able to vent his true feelings. He clawed at Henry's shoulders and clenched around his finger without thought. By the time the waves of orgasm subsided, Henry had his body wedged fully between Kellen's legs and the pressure in Kellen's ass had grown. There was more than one finger in him now.

Henry released Kellen's spent cock and sat back on his heels. He thrust in and out of Kellen's ass a few times before pulling out. When he returned, the fingers were slicker still and there were three of them. With the orgasm over, unease made Kellen tighten again.

Henry rubbed his palm over Kellen's abdomen. "Easy, darling. Try to relax. That's it," he encouraged as he slowly pushed his fingers in, deeper each time, before sliding them almost all the way out. "That's it. Slow, even breaths. There's no hurry. I need you to be fully prepared before I mount you." He scraped against that spot again.

Kellen arched his back. "Oh! What is that?"

"Just a little thing the physicians call a prostate. All men have one, and although it's not clear what its benefit is for our health, it makes this kind of lovemaking for a man marvelously enjoyable."

Kellen moaned and tossed his head from side-to-side. "It's almost too much." He could feel his dick hardening already. With the intensity of the pleasure, he couldn't keep his eyes open. *Next time.* He wanted to be able to see his husband.

"Good boy," Henry crooned at the point in which Kellen was both aroused and relaxed.

Henry pulled his fingers out and pushed Kellen's knees up. He then clasped Kellen's dick once more and jerked it. The climax was building again inside Kellen, so much so that he nearly missed how something else was trying to press into his hole. The moment he realized he was about to be breached, he couldn't help tensing once more.

"Easy." Henry jerked him harder, an excellent effort at distraction. The blunt head of the man's cock merely rubbed around the puckered ring. "Push out, darling. I know it makes no sense, but it will ease my passage."

His head clouded by his arousal, Kellen struggled to make sense of his husband's words. He tried to do as he said, but the rush of another orgasm jumbled his thoughts even more. And as he groaned and writhed his way through the climax, pain invaded his ass. It made him tense more, even as the orgasm tried to stupefy him.

Kellen whimpered and tried to pull away. "Too much, too much. It hurts!"

The pain receded immediately, and Kellen found himself wrapped in his husband's arms.

Henry stroked his face. "Shh. Easy, darling. I'm out now. Better?"

Kellen nodded, relieved that the unpleasant ache was waning, but also ashamed that he couldn't do the one thing in particular that he'd both dreamed of and needed to do to satisfy his husband and the law. Burying his face in the man's chest, he let the tears flow. "I'm sorry."

"What's this?" Henry parted them with his hand gently cupping Kellen's chin. "Why are you crying and apologizing? You've done nothing wrong, Kellen."

Kellen tried to get himself under control in order to answer coherently. "Mounting me is your right and what we need to do to consummate our marriage." Despite his efforts, the tears returned, harder than ever.

Henry gathered him close and ran his hand up and down Kellen's back. "Kellen, please don't cry. What you've said is simply not true. My only right, when it comes to your body, is to do whatever you give me permission to do. I may be your lord when it comes to matters of society, but in our bed, we are equals. You have your own agency. Do you understand? And," he continued before Kellen could muster any kind of reply, "what we do here is between us. No one gets to say whether our marriage has been consummated or not except us. We are married, well and truly. Please never doubt that."

Kellen couldn't suppress the shudders as he worked to regain control and stop the crying. "But mounting me is what you want, isn't it? I don't want to disappoint you."

His husband let out a bark of laughter. "Oh, darling, that's impossible. Having you here, pressed against me, seeing your face when I make you come and knowing that I can protect you with my name gives me the greatest happiness I've ever known."

Those words filled him with a measure of pride and helped to ease his worry—almost. He was still determined to let his husband fill his ass, but before he could open his mouth to say so, Henry grabbed Kellen's hand and pressed it against the hard, warm length lying between them.

He covered it with his own. "See what you do to me?" Henry led Kellen in jerking the taut shaft. It didn't take more than a few tugs before the man groaned and bucked against their hold. Warm cum splashed over Kellen's fingers, and Henry's harsh breath blew the strands of his hair.

When it was over, his husband rose briefly to lower the flame of the one lantern in the room, then pulled the covers up to their chins and continued to hug Kellen close. "We need sleep. In the morning, we'll return to the camp and discuss the next steps. For now, wife, please put all worries out of your head and get some rest. Wake me if you become cold during the night, however, and I will refill the bedwarmers."

It was impossible to be anything other than toasty warm with Henry's large body wrapped around him. And the reminder of what he was expected to do now that he was the Baroness of Roth caused his stomach to clench. He hated the idea of leading Henry's men into the castle to force the end of the siege. But he had to trust his husband when he promised to shed as little blood as possible. He knew, though, that his father and sister wouldn't surrender easily, or at all, and feared that within a few days' time, the castle floor would run red.

* * * *

Kellen roused from his sleep slowly, languidly, not quite awake yet unable to drift off again. He was hot and aroused, as was the man pressed against him.

Henry's hard cock dug into Kellen's stomach, proof of his husband's virility. Kellen instinctively nudged closer, his need to be plastered against Henry overriding his normal reticence. He pushed so hard that Henry rolled onto his back with only a sigh. Keeping his eyes shut and letting his mind continue to wander in and out of consciousness, Kellen followed him and lay on top of the larger body.

Their dicks brushed, making Kellen's jerk and his hole clench. Henry's low moan sounded like an invitation. Kellen didn't allow himself to think — he just *did* — pushing up to a sitting position, using Henry's chest for leverage. Then he slid up so that he sat directly against his husband's cock. With one last effort to stay calm and sleepy, he lifted the shaft up and pressed it against his hole. He lowered himself onto it, ignoring the burning as the massive cock stretched him wide. Remnants of the oil Henry had applied eased the way, but Kellen was determined to take it all, regardless. Remembering his husband's advice, he pushed out as the dick slowly snaked up his ass. He didn't stop until he was fully seated, hanging his head and taking in deep breaths as he accommodated the invasion. Being filled was uncomfortable, but the pain he'd experienced the first time was gone. Now all he felt was a fullness that, while strange, wasn't unpleasant. In fact, he appreciated the way it pressed against his prostate and finally understood why men liked being mounted.

"Darling." Henry's voice was sleepy, and he clasped Kellen by the waist. "What are you doing? You'll hurt yourself." He tried to lift Kellen off.

Kellen resisted and pressed down even more. "I want this, Henry. I want *you*."

Only vaguely aware of what to do, Kellen braced his palms once more on his husband's chest and began to rock. When that movement proved to be more pleasant than uncomfortable, he increased his efforts by posting up and down Henry's cock. He went slowly at first, but with each pass, he began to feel true pleasure. His dick rose, and Henry immediately grabbed it. He jerked the shaft in sync with Kellen's riding.

Kellen felt the orgasm rise within him, and the intensity that having Henry inside added to the experience was indescribable. At the same time, Henry's dick swelled inside Kellen's ass. They came together, each groaning and shuddering. A splash of warmth coated his channel and knowing that he'd done that for his husband, made his own cock convulse even more. When there was no more cum left to release by either of them, Kellen stopped moving and flopped onto his husband.

The man cupped Kellen's ass cheek with one hand and gently eased his deflating cock out of Kellen. "I believe I'd like to wake up every morning in such a manner."

Elated by his achievement, Kellen blew out a chuckle. "I can't promise anything, husband, but I'll do my best."

"That's all I ask." He paused. "Are you all right?"

"More than."

Henry squeezed gently. "I mean are you sore?"

Kellen tested his answer by squeezing his sphincter. "Some, but in a good way, if that makes sense."

"It does. I hate thinking that you took the chance of trying this just to please me."

Kellen kissed the side of his husband's throat. "There was no planning in this, no rational decision. I woke wanting you, and the rest came naturally." He lifted his head. It was nearly impossible to see any part of his husband's face in the gloom. "I regret nothing. Having you inside me gave me the most amazing orgasm. I can't wait to do it again." He meant it now that there was no question his body could accommodate Henry's dick with proper relaxation as well as prepping.

"I will take you at your word, wife. You must always tell me the truth."

Kellen almost took that directive to heart and blurted out that which was lodged deeply in his heart now. *I love you.* He held his tongue literally by biting it. Such a grandiose expression of his feelings was probably not something his soldier husband needed, or even wanted, to hear. On their short acquaintance, it made no sense to love the man, anyway. Perhaps in the future, he would find the time to admit how he felt, and maybe if he were really fortunate, Henry would love him back. That was probably asking for too much and he knew better than to raise his own hopes. It would be enough if they could make a nice, companionable life with each other. And their compatibility in bed was now confirmed.

A disturbing thought popped into his mind, however. "Will you…?"

"What?"

"Take lovers?" He really had no right to ask such a question. Powerful people took anyone they wanted into their beds. It was the way of things. His father and siblings had always taken whomever they desired. Even when Kellen's mother and Wilford had been alive, the duke and his heir thought nothing of the sensibilities of their wives. Fidelity among the nobility was not a given.

Henry took so long to answer that Kellen started to take the words back.

"No. I won't. My vows included cherishing you. Taking lovers when I have a wife would be churlish of me. Besides, since my first sight of you, I've wanted no one else."

"Really?"

"Don't sound so surprised, darling. You really are ignorant of your own worth. I intend to change the misperception on a daily basis. I'm only sorry I have no ring to give you. When I have a chance, I'll see if the village has anything worthy to buy."

Warmed by his husband's words and satisfied with this assurance, at least, he told himself the love part was of no importance. "I don't need one, truly."

"You shall have one, nevertheless. I want the world to know you're mine."

"Will you wear one, too?" he dared to ask.

"If it pleases you, I will."

"Thank you. I want the world to know you belong to me, as well." He yawned loudly. "Oh, forgive me. I could use some more sleep if possible."

"The dawn has not yet broken, so yes, go back to sleep."

On a sigh, Kellen did as he was told, more content than he'd ever been before.

Chapter Eleven

Henry couldn't help but check on his wife often as they made their way back to the encampment. The boy had to find riding uncomfortable after the night they'd spent. It had been a time of extreme emotions — from the deep-seated fear that he'd hurt Kellen when trying to breach him to the unparalleled delight of waking to find his wife riding his dick. He would have waited as long as it took to make Kellen comfortable with being mounted. The courage it had taken for the boy to initiate and succeed in the act was astounding. The more time he spent with the duke's son, the more he admired him. And his feelings were growing, too. The way his heart tripped every time he looked at the beautiful boy, it convinced him more that he was indeed falling in love. It had to be so. Nothing else could make him happy and scared at the same time.

Can I really make a life with him? Will he ever love me back?

He'd rather face a legion of soldiers single-handedly than contemplate a life where his wife merely tolerated him — or even hated him. What happened next as he led his soldiers to invade Highrock would reveal all to him. If he couldn't keep the death on the Duke of Cragmore's side low, Kellen might never forgive him, married or not.

When he could see the camp, he kicked his horse into a fast trot. The others, Kellen included, did the same, and Henry winced inwardly at how he was probably making the ride harder for his wife's body. But he couldn't think of only the boy's comfort or his own desire to pamper his wife. What mattered was planning the right method to breach the castle and end the siege. Colin had been working on a plan but only in the abstract. They still didn't know how to get in. Now that he and Kellen were wed, he hoped the boy would be forthcoming without delay.

They reached the paddock for the camp. Henry kept an eye on his wife's dismount and was pleased to see no evidence of pain. Better still, Kellen approached him without needing to be asked and said the words Henry had been hoping to hear.

"We should go to your tent so that I can tell you what I know, and we can plan your entry into Highrock." Closing his eyes briefly, he added, "I hope I'm doing the right thing."

Henry cupped his wife's face with both hands. "You are." He placed a kiss on the boy's forehead for good measure and took his hand to lead him through the camp.

Everyone stopped what they were doing and watched them go by, mostly in silence. It was a bit unnerving for so much attention to be on them. Not for his own sake, but because he didn't want Kellen to feel embarrassed or unwelcome. Henry pulled the boy closer and stared down anyone who looked like they held any ill-will. He wouldn't tolerate any disrespect for his wife. Fortunately, familiar faces of the men he'd trained and fought with personally were there to greet them, and they showed not only respect, but a certain amount of affection. One grizzled soldier even dared to wink at him.

Then there was Colin, waiting for them outside Henry's tent. The bannerman nodded his head. "Welcome back, my lord. Greetings to you, Baroness," he added. As always, the man had a bit of a twinkle in his eyes, not taking much seriously outside of battle. But he obviously approved of the marriage in fact and not merely in theory. Knowing he had at least one person he could rely on when it came to Kellen relieved a tension in Henry that he'd been carrying since leaving the abbey.

"Summon the council. We have plans to make."

"Right away, Hal."

Henry led Kellen inside the tent—one that Henry barely recognized. All his things were there, but there was more. And the *more* was prettier than his drab stuff. The covering of his bed had been changed to a brightly colored blue comforter with a threaded design of flowers. Seat cushions of similar hue and elaborateness sat on the chairs, and beside his own clothes, lay a neat pile of new ones. Arrangements of dried flowers stuck into glass vases stood on the tables. The whole place smelled like a fresh meadow, even though winter was stripping the landscape of color.

His wife gasped as he took in the new décor. "Oh, how lovely!"

Frederic appeared out of nowhere. "Do you like it, my lady?" The boy frowned. "Should I call you 'my lady' or is it 'my lord'?"

Kellen shrugged as he went to peruse his new clothing. "It matters not to me. If the baron is 'my lord', I suppose you should stick with 'my lady' for me. It's less confusing that way." He turned around. "I can't thank you enough for all this."

Frederic blushed, a most unusual thing for a squire to do. "It was nothing, my lady. I thought you'd enjoy coming home to a freshened and prettier tent."

"Well, it was a lovely thought. Thank you again." Kellen put his hand to his stomach. "I'm a bit hungry from our ride, and I assume my husband is even more so. Might we have our luncheon early?"

"Of course! I'll fetch it right away."

"Best make it for the entire council, lad," Henry said. "We're meeting soon and will be at it for hours."

Frederic nodded. "Yes, my lord."

Henry went to Kellen and kissed him on the lips — only once. It was hard to show such restraint, but with the men arriving at any moment, he didn't want to embarrass his wife. "Are you truly happy with the redecorating?"

Kellen looked as if he might follow Henry's lips for another kiss. "Of course, I am. Aren't you?"

Henry backed up to put space between them, loving the mewl of disappointment in his wife's expression. "I don't much care what my tent looks like. I only want you to be happy."

"I am." Kellen's simple answer was more reassuring than anything more effusive might be.

Henry dared to ask a more important question while they were still alone. "How are you feeling? Does anything hurt that you might want the doctor to help with?"

Now it was Kellen who blushed. He rolled his eyes. "I'm fine," he said in a low voice.

Just as well, because before Henry could question him further, his council of advisors entered. Each one of them greeted both him and his wife with the usual courtesy. None of them showed any outward curiosity, probably because Colin was clear on the matter of the new baroness and had already answered any question they might have had. Kellen was the way to end the siege, and that fact alone overpowered all other considerations.

Henry led Kellen to take the chair next to his and sat at the head of the table. Colin sat on the other side and the others ranged themselves around as they usually did. Sir Robert unfurled a map of the area and used stones to hold down each corner. No one said anything, waiting for Henry to start the meeting.

He placed his hand on his wife's shoulder. "Where is the entry point, Baroness?" He wanted to use an endearment, but it wasn't the time or place, and a reminder of Kellen's new status couldn't hurt.

Kellen didn't answer right away. Instead, he stared at the map, deep in his own thoughts. After a while, Henry feared the boy would balk at revealing what he knew now that the time had come. He needn't have doubted his wife. Kellen rose and leaning over the table, placed his finger on a spot.

Everyone stared at it with varying degrees of surprise.

Henry wasn't at all. He'd suspected as much all along. "The shore."

Kellen nodded as he sat back down. "When the tide is out, that's how one can leave the castle undetected — and how you can get in."

* * * *

Henry took a moment to bask in the silence after the others had left. The planning of the invasion of the castle had lasted well into the evening, and as excited as he was for the end of the siege to be in sight, what he really wanted now was some peace and quiet with his wife. And it wasn't simply a desire to bed Kellen again. The boy was sitting in his usual chair by the brazier, staring at the carpet while he sipped a glass of wine. One didn't have to be a long-married husband to see how much his wife suffered with what he'd done.

"You are saving your people from a long winter of deprivation," he said as he grabbed his own glass and went to join Kellen.

"I know." Kellen didn't look up as Henry sat beside him. "You weren't surprised by the location of the secret passage." It wasn't a question.

Henry sighed inwardly. "No."

"You thought it was there all along. That's why you took me riding on the beach." The boy's tone was weary more than accusatory.

Because he believed in honesty between a married couple, Henry answered with the truth. "Yes, I had hoped you'd give something away by accident if not directly. I can't apologize for it, darling. My duty is to my king and men. This siege dragging on benefits no one."

Kellen glanced his way. Gods, but the boy looked tired. "I've learned to hide my thoughts and feelings. It wasn't hard to keep from giving anything away." He took another sip of wine. "Why did you think it was there?"

Henry shrugged. "It was the most logical location. It's the farthest away from where any attacking army could make camp, and one can walk along the coast without being seen. Plus, the boy who tried to kill me had dried salt on the hem of his trousers. It was obviously from sea water. That confirmed my suspicions, no matter your behavior when we were there."

"You're very clever, my lord." The words were spoken without mocking or admiration—simply stating the truth.

Henry stared into his wine. "It's the reason the king trusted me with this problem. He also knows that my temperament is such that I won't let my men go on a killing spree. We'll take the castle with as little fighting as possible. Anyone unarmed or who lays down their weapons will be spared. You have my word on that, Kellen."

Now his wife looked at him. "I have no doubt of that, Henry. I wouldn't have agreed to marry you and provide you with the information you needed if I thought you couldn't be trusted to take the castle with compassion and restraint. Besides," he continued with a brief smile, "I'll be there to remind you of it, if need be."

Surprised, although he probably shouldn't have been, Henry straightened and stared his wife in his eyes. "You will *not* be there, darling. Here you will stay, far from the fighting and well-guarded, should any of your father's men escape with vengeance on their minds."

"I'm not staying here. I'm going with you." Kellen's expression and tone indicated that this had been his assumption all along and that anything to the contrary was simply wrong.

Henry strived for patience. "Darling, you are not a soldier, and even if you were, I'd still not permit you to come. There is no reason to put your life in danger, nor make you fight your own family."

Tossing back the rest of his wine, Kellen slammed his glass on the table between them, stood and began to pace. "I may not be a fighting man, but I do have training and do passably well using a long knife. And my presence might give my father's people reason to surrender. Most of them are not fanatically devoted to him."

"I'm glad to hear it, but you're still not going. You must trust that I can be persuasive to those interested in living instead of dying for the duke's doomed cause."

Kellen planted himself in front of Henry, his hands on his hips and fire in his eyes. "You need me to lead the way through the escape tunnels. They are deliberately designed to confuse invaders."

Momentarily distracted by how fetching his wife was when angry, it took Henry a few seconds to respond. "You can draw us a map."

"I've only been through them a few times, mostly as a child for fun. I won't remember which turns to make until I see them again."

Henry finished his wine and set the glass beside his wife's. He liked the way they looked side-by-side, the normality of it. "We'll muddle through. Now, we must retire. Tomorrow comes early, and I have much to do to ready my men before we make our move at nightfall." He tried to take his wife by the arm.

Kellen evaded his touch and stalked over to his side of the bed. He began to strip with angry motions. "If you were so sure of where the entrance was and being able to do this without my help, why bother to marry me?"

Henry allowed himself the pleasure of watching his wife reveal his lovely skin bit by bit. It was the only thing he was going to get to enjoy, he was sure, that night. He may as well give himself permission to ogle.

Kellen stopped in the middle of undoing the laces to his trousers. "What?"

Henry shook his head. "Nothing." He started removing his own clothes. "But to answer your question, finding the exact location would have been difficult and besides, marrying you served another purpose."

Kellen stood naked, even his small clothes removed. "And what was that?"

Henry winced as he pushed his trousers past his erection. "Being my wife gives you protection. If I don't...return from the fighting, you will be well-cared for. As Baroness Roth, you will be entitled to an escort back to Rothberg and will have access to a significant income that will provide for you the rest of your life."

Kellen gasped. "You think that's what I'm worried about?" Fury vibrated in his voice, and his eyes spit fire.

Henry slipped under the covers to hide his arousal. That last thing his wife would want was his attention this night. "If you're not, you should be." He closed his eyes briefly and sighed. "Whatever happens, I don't want you under your father's thumb again. There is no chance of that now, regardless of the outcome. You deserve this future, Kellen."

"I'm thinking about everyone's future, Henry. Your success depends on gaining access to the castle quickly and quietly. I know where the tunnel leads and how best to go from that point to the bailey while avoiding detection. Without me, you'll surely have to fight your way to open the gates. A lot of blood will be shed with a more uncertain outcome. You know I'm right, Henry."

Regrettably, what the boy said made sense. But Kellen wasn't just any boy. He was Henry's wife. "You're not coming." He made his tone as firm as possible.

"Oh, you're insufferable!"

"I'm sure you're right about that, darling." He started to lie down. "Damn, the lamps."

"Don't bother to get up. I'll turn them down."

A better husband would have insisted on doing the chore himself. Henry was not that, apparently, because he benefited from the selfishness too much. Kellen stomped around the tent dousing the light, his pale beauty on full display. This was the first time he was able to look at all of his wife with impunity, and the view was spectacular. His cock pulsed with need, and his balls cramped with the desire to empty into that beckoning ass.

Knowing that they would all have to be disappointed, Henry settled into the bed and closed his eyes when the last of the light was snuffed out. Kellen crawled under the covers and lay beside him. The boy's proximity was torture. Henry doubted he'd sleep at all in his unfulfilled state.

Kellen huffed. "So now you're mad at me?"

Surprised, Henry popped his eyes open. "I'm not mad, darling."

"Finished with me, then."

Confused, Henry asked, "Why do you think that?"

"Because you're not touching me. Now that you have all the information you needed, you want nothing more to do with me."

Henry nearly laughed at the absurd statement. Liking his balls right where they were, however, he didn't infuriate his wife more. Instead, he turned to face the boy. "You're entirely wrong about that. If you need proof, give me your hand."

Kellen actually did as he asked. And when it was in reach, Henry tugged it over to touch his hard dick. Then, his point made, he didn't wait for any more talk. He tugged Kellen closer and wrapped his arm around him. When his cock bumped against his wife's hip, he had to bite back a groan.

"Of course I want you, wife. I just assumed you are angry with me and aren't interested in having me ask for sex."

"It's what married people do, isn't it, even if they are fighting?"

"I have no idea. This is my first time being a husband, and it never occurred to me to ask married men of my acquaintance whether their wives welcome them in bed if they are at odds with each other. Besides, what other people do is not the point. Do you want me to make love to you?" He didn't question using the gentler expression for having sex. It seemed right and proper.

Kellen took a moment to answer. "I think I should say no, but that wouldn't be true. As mad as I am, I still crave having you inside me."

Henry nearly came right then and there, hearing that bald, yet obviously sincere, confession. He gritted his teeth until he had his dick under control. "You must be sore, darling. We can do other things."

Kellen gripped his cock tightly. "No, I'm not. And it doesn't matter, anyway. I've been thinking about this all day. I want you to beach me and be in control. Fuck me, Henry. *Please.*"

Henry doubted there was any man alive who could resist such a demand from his wife. He certainly didn't have the self-control, and under the circumstances, there didn't seem a need to. Kellen was the best judge of his own condition, and if he proved to be wrong about that, Henry would have to be extra alert to signs of pain and stop.

He gave Kellen a good, long kiss before leaving the bed. With the moonlight shining through the smoke hole, he had no trouble maneuvering around the tent and locating the pot of cream he'd asked Frederic for in a private moment. It was thicker than the oil in the abbey had been, and he intended to go even more slowly than he had the night before.

Rejoining his wife, he got right down to it. As he kissed Kellen again, he spread the boy's legs and bent his knees. Then settling between them, he coated one finger with the cream and slid it past the boy's hole. Unlike the first time, his wife didn't need as much prolonged preparation as he'd expected. The puckered ring gave him no resistance. It became loose and pliant immediately. The little moan Kellen murmured into Henry's mouth confirmed that the invasion was welcome.

He'd still intended to take things slowly. His wife had other ideas. It was Kellen who deepened the kiss and demanded more by clawing at his arms and bucking his hips. Henry progressed to two fingers, then three, each time finding welcome. He scraped against Kellen's prostate and swallowed his cry as he came without Henry needing to touch his cock at all. The responsiveness of this boy was remarkable.

Kellen broke the kiss and panted his way through his climax. "More, Henry. All of you."

Henry was resistant to the idea of breaching his wife with his cock already, but Kellen's insistence wasn't to be ignored. Coating his dick as much as possible with cream, Henry replaced his fingers with it. He pushed only the tip of his cock in. There was no resistance, so he continued to slide his cock inside, slowly, looking for signs that his wife was hurting.

Kellen was having none of it. Bending his knees nearly to his ears, the boy bucked his hips to engulf Henry's dick. Then he squeezed his hole, and Henry was lost.

He braced his hands on either side of his wife's head and thrust in deep. When his wife simply moaned and murmured breathless encouragement, he picked up the pace, fucking with long and ever-faster thrusts, rolling his hips forward and up with each pass. His climax built quickly, and he didn't even try to hold it back. With a jerk, his dick erupted. He didn't stop until his balls were empty and he couldn't hold himself up any longer. He collapsed on top of his wife, knowing that he, too, had come again. They lay entangled until Henry gathered the strength to roll off the boy.

Kellen snuggled into his embrace. "I will always want you, Henry. And I'm coming with you."

Henry gave in as he imagined men everywhere did. "Fine." He closed his eyes and willed himself to sleep.

* * * *

Kellen tugged the sides of his cloak closer in defense against the bitter winds whipping along the shore. Not knowing the exact timing of the tide going out, he and the others had been waiting a while now, hunkered against the dunes and watching for their opportunity. The sun had been down for a long time, and with the darkness of the moonless night and the angle of the castle, they were as unlikely to be seen by the castle sentries as possible. There was a chance, though, that someone had spotted their approach to the beach or the fact that Henry's men were amassed closer to the gate. There were no assurances in war. Still, he prayed that they would all get in undetected and end the fighting quickly.

The long knife he wore on his belt made him feel more secure, even as he dreaded the idea of having to use it. Henry had been excruciatingly clear on how Kellen was to stick behind him and stay out of the fighting. Kellen had no intention of disobeying his husband on that point. His intention had never been to be part of the force to take the castle. His insistence on being a part of the invasion was in the hope that he could broker the fastest conclusion to the siege as possible. He owed it to both Henry and his family to at least try.

The nose plate on the helmet he was wearing made it hard to see. He shifted it some, but it was too big for him to wear comfortably. At least Henry hadn't made him wear a breastplate. None of the extra ones they had in camp had fit his small size, and they'd dared not try to find one in the village. The fewer people who knew what was happening, the better. He didn't really think he was at risk of being killed, anyway. No one in the castle had a reason to target him specifically.

"If you take that off, I'll lay you across my lap and beat that pretty ass of yours." Henry's voice was low to keep it private between the two of them.

Kellen huffed and tried to glare at his husband. The helmet made it impossible for him to show his displeasure, however. "I have no intention of that, my lord, as I am not stupid. And if you dare to strike me, I'll blacken your eye."

Henry uttered a sound that might have been a laugh. "You can certainly try, darling." The infuriating man's helmet fit him perfectly, the hard steel framing his face and covering his nose, giving him a menacing look of raw power. Anyone meeting him in battle should drop to their knees in surrender. "You know," he continued before Kellen could reply, "there are those who find a bit of spanking to be quite arousing."

"I can't imagine why," Kellen retorted, although even as he did, his hole clenched with surprising interest.

Henry came to alert. "It is time. The tide is out enough." He signaled to his men and led the way.

With his heart thumping wildly, Kellen followed.

Chapter Twelve

It had been years since Kellen had walked through the escape tunnel. To his knowledge, it had never been used as intended before. He wondered briefly if anyone in the castle was already planning their escape when the siege ended in favor of the king. No one was there to block them when they'd splashed through the retreating surf into the mouth of what appeared to be a natural cave. As far as he knew, it was. One of his ancestors had managed to carve the tunnels deep under the castle to connect to what the gods had already put there.

He led the way, sort of. Henry was a few steps ahead of him as he directed the man which way to go. Sir Robert was by his other side, sticking to him closely, as undoubtedly he'd been commanded to. Kellen hadn't been lying to Henry about his usefulness. There were false paths laid down, tricky because they gave the illusion of going up when in fact, they merely dead-ended. The true paths appeared to slope downward until one went far enough. They sloped upward, steadily cutting deeper into the cliff upon which the castle had been built.

A couple of times, Kellen had to stop to remember. It became easier the farther they went. Rock quickly turned into packed dirt, braced by timber. The air became thicker, but also warmer. Kellen really wanted to shed his helmet and his cloak but dared not. Henry had been clear on this point, and Kellen understood that a soldier had to be ready for battle at any moment. By the time they reached the access to the castle, however, Kellen was wet with sweat. His heart pounded with fear, as well. With the battle upon them, he was truly scared, not for himself, but for Henry...and everyone else. Despite his father's cruel indifference to him and his sister's open contempt, he didn't want them to die.

Henry stopped in front of the huge wooden door and held up his hand for everyone to step back. Kellen had told them that it opened up to the wine cellar. At this time of night, supper would be well underway in the great hall. All the needed drink should have been collected already, so no servant should be there. Still, there would certainly be guards of some sort. His father was madly ambitious but not stupid. This tunnel was a liability to the castle's safety as much as a means of escape.

Henry pressed his ear to the door, then beckoned to four soldiers standing behind Kellen. The men stepped past him, drawing their swords as they joined their leader. Kellen couldn't recall whether the hinges squeaked or not. It didn't matter. There would be no hiding the fact that it was shoved open. The benefit of surprise worked to Henry's favor. Kellen had to stand on tiptoe, peering over Sir Robert's shoulder to see what was happening. It was over quickly with little noise. When he was finally permitted to enter, he saw two young guards, bound and gagged, and shoved into a corner.

Kellen sagged with relief. Henry had kept his promise to spare those who surrendered from death, as these two apparently had. Kellen wanted to go to reassure them that all would be well. One look from Henry told him he wouldn't be allowed to, so putting the idea aside, he continued to give his husband the benefit of his presence. He led them around the winding racks of wine to the next door that opened into a hallway connecting the kitchen to the rest of the castle.

Once again, he was pushed aside, Sir Robert's hand on his shoulder in case he was foolish enough to rush forward and do...what? *Doesn't Henry trust me?* He knew the answer. As much as his husband showed him great respect and affection, he still didn't know for sure where Kellen's loyalties lay. Plus, he'd lectured Kellen endlessly on how he wasn't to put himself in danger, no matter the temptation to do otherwise. Kellen had no intention of doing so, except that if he thought it would help his husband, he wasn't sure he'd be able to adhere to his promise.

Because the kitchen was the fastest route to the gates, Henry led his men in that direction. The people there were ordinary servants, powerless in matters of state, and forced to obey their lord, no matter how they felt. Even so, the instinct to protect oneself and one's home led some of them to try to fight with what they had to hand or flee. Henry's men were no match for them, however. They easily disarmed those who wielded butcher knives, ladles or rolling pins, and caught the pages who'd run to the door leading to the bailey. The fights were quick, leaving some unconscious and dragged to the back of the kitchen where the others were being herded. They were made to sit, with the resistors being tied as well.

Henry surprised him by beckoning him forward. "Reassure them," he said in a low voice.

Knowing that the cook was the one person the others would look to, Kellen went to the woman and knelt in front of where she sat glaring, a rope immobilizing her large hands on her lap. "Please stay quiet, Mistress Hortense. Baron Roth is not interested in massacring all of you. He wants to end the siege, that is all."

The woman's expression slowly softened. "The duke was ever an ass and you a kindly boy. We'll do as you ask. Please don't make us regret it."

Putting his hand against his heart, he said, "I promise."

Relieved, Kellen rose and followed Henry to the next part of their journey. This was where it became particularly difficult. The soldiers guarding the bailey would fight out of reflex, if nothing else. And while Henry had brought a couple of dozen soldiers with him, it wasn't enough to intimidate anyone into surrendering. The gates had to be opened to let the hundreds of soldiers quietly amassed outside to enter. When they reached the outside door, two young soldiers came forward, their swords sheathed.

Henry nodded at them. "You know what to do."

The boys nodded back, although the baron hadn't asked a question. Their quiet courage was inspiring. This is where the entire venture could fall apart.

Kellen managed to push into a position to watch as Henry opened the door, and the boys flew out. Archers stepped up with arrows notched. As the boys sped toward the gate, the archers loosed their arrows to fell the duke's men as they realized what was happening and tried to stop the runners. The archers went out into the bailey and others filled in the gaps. Some aimed high to target the soldiers on the ramparts while the others took out the ones pouring out of the guardhouse once the alarm bell pealed. Kellen had read enough about history to know what the plan was. Henry had picked messengers to race toward their goal without stopping to defend themselves. They counted on the protection of others, and while they had to dodge some of the duke's men, as well as arrows striking the ground in their pathway, they didn't waver from their goal.

Grabbing the ropes at the portcullis, the boys showed enviable strength as they pulled to open the gate. Henry's men poured through it before it was fully raised. Sir Colin led the charge, of course. He was Henry's bannerman, and like the baron, led from the front, instead of staying behind the lines. Soldiers from the barracks and the castle arrived, and the fighting began in earnest. With no power to influence this part, Kellen stood clasping his hands, anxiously tracking Henry's movements.

His husband fought his way up to the ramparts. Then he grabbed an alarm horn from one of his men and blew. "Lay down your arms. Surrender and quarter will be given." He shouted, but it was hard to be heard over the din of fighting. He blew the horn again and repeated his command.

Slowly, his father's men started to drop their weapons, raise their arms and drop to their knees. As well-trained as they were, none of Henry's soldiers took advantage of them. They'd been ordered to accept the surrender and secure the fighters as much as possible. Kellen braced himself against the doorjamb with relief. The plan had worked—almost. There was more to be done.

Henry came running down the stairs. As he passed Kellen, he barked, "Stay here."

Knowing that his husband headed for the great room, and therefore, his father and sister, Kellen wasn't about to stay away, even if his husband commanded it. He hoped he might have sway over his family, despite a lifetime of disrespect. He managed to evade Sir Robert's grasp and race after Henry.

Inside, it was eerily quiet. A few dozens of the duke's men stood with swords raised, guarding the old man sitting at the high table. Chairs were knocked over and food was strewn everywhere, testament to how his father's men had been taken by surprise. One of the soldiers ran toward Henry with his sword raised and a war cry screeching out of his mouth. Kellen's heart stopped for a moment, and he gasped. There was no reason to worry, however. Henry dispatched the man quickly and stood with his legs braced as he faced the duke from afar.

"It is over, Cragmore. Tell your men to lay down their weapons."

The duke stood, strong and steady despite his age. He sneered at Henry. "So, Roth, you managed to invade my home…through my brat's treachery, I see." His gaze slid past Henry and bored into Kellen.

Not so long ago, that stare would have made Kellen's knees weak and his stomach clench. With Henry steps away from him, that fear was gone. He lifted his chin and glared back at his father.

"You are speaking of my wife, your grace." Henry's tone was colder than the coming winter. "And you should thank Kellen for helping to end this siege without your people starving to death or being slaughtered."

The tension grew as the duke made no move and gave no response. Finally, with a narrowed gaze and look of hatred, he motioned for his men to put down their weapons. It didn't take much to convince them. The clatter of steel on stone filled the room. Henry's shoulders relaxed in a way that would only be noticeable if one were watching and knew the man as well as Kellen now did. It was remarkable to think that only a few days ago, he'd been fleeing from this man, then waging a war of words with him.

It's over. Except... Kellen took a step forward. "Where's Isolde?"

He'd no more uttered that question, when a movement from the balcony on the second floor caught his eye. His sister raised her longbow with an arrow notched. Her target was clear.

"No!" Kellen screamed and ran to Henry. He threw himself in front of his husband without thought, and as the pain knocked him to the floor, he could only be happy that it did.

Henry's world tilted, nearly knocking him off his feet until he managed to get himself under control. The moment he did, he dropped his sword and tore off his helmet. Then he knelt by his wife, working to control a feeling of horror greater than any he'd known. He removed Kellen's helmet with great care and stared down at this beautiful face. Thank the gods the boy was still breathing. He castigated himself, however, that he hadn't risked having armor made to fit his wife's slender form. Isolde had been aiming for Henry's exposed groin. By putting himself between Henry and the arrow, Kellen had allowed it to pierce his chest through the gambeson.

"Darling."

Kellen's eyelids fluttered open. "I love you," was all he said before they closed again.

Henry cupped his cheek. "Stay with me, wife. When you're better, I'll show you just how much I feel the same way."

Sir Robert joined them. "I'm sorry, my lord. He escaped me."

Henry couldn't help but smile as he swept back Kellen's sweaty hair. "You'll find my wife can be very stubborn. Fetch the doctor." He had to work to keep the panic from his voice."

The second Robert left, Colin replaced him. "Everyone is being secured, Hal."

"Not everyone. Find that woman."

"Count on it."

"And I want her alive," he shouted after his friend.

With that chore tended to, he refocused on his wife. He really wanted to pull the offending arrow out of the boy's precious body, but he knew better. Men were known to bleed out if it were done improperly. It seemed like forever before Allen came. He knelt on his bony knees, seemingly indifferent to the hard stone floor.

The doctor narrowed his gaze, then nodded. "It doesn't appear to have pierced his heart or his lungs. Break the shaft and we'll tend to the rest in your tent. He needs warmth and some of the cordial."

Henry nodded, relieved beyond measure and carefully cut the shaft of the arrow himself. Then he lifted his wife and cradled him against his chest. "Hang on, darling. You're going to be fine. I promise."

* * * *

Henry's father had once told him that hearing his wife's screams as she labored to deliver their children had cut deeper than any wound he'd ever born in battle. One's own pain paled in comparison to seeing someone you love experiencing it. And now Henry knew that to be true himself. Watching Doctor Allen remove the arrowhead from Kellen's delicate body, leaving his pale skin bathed in red, had made Henry want to scream and break things—Isolde's neck being the primary choice.

The doctor stood back from the bed. Kellen lay under the covers, still unconscious but breathing normally. "All is well, my lord. The baroness was lucky. I won't deny that."

Henry put his hand on the man's shoulder. "I cannot thank you enough."

The man waved that declaration away and packed up his bag. "I've left more cordial on the table mixed with an analgesic...the same as I did for you. He should take a spoonful every few hours, even if he doesn't wake. Get it down him. It's important for him to be dosed frequently for the next few days."

Henry nodded. "I'll see it done." He wanted to sit on the bed, but understanding that it might hurt Kellen to do so, he had to be content with dragging a chair over to the side. He settled down and stared at his wife as he slept. He knew the moment Colin entered.

"How is he?" his friend asked in a low voice.

"He was lucky," Henry responded, echoing the doctor's words. "What is the status of the castle?"

"It's secure. All the higher-ranked soldiers of the duke have been locked in the dungeon. We'll need to sort out who can be trusted at some point, but so far, everyone is being compliant. The duke and Lady Isolde are confined to their rooms."

Henry made a fist. "I half wanted her to resist so that you'd be forced to kill her. She must pay for what she's done, but I'm cowardly enough to not want her blood on my hands. No matter what the justification, I don't think my wife could ever forgive me for it."

"For what it's worth, she appears genuinely upset that she hit her brother instead of you. I believe she can be…rehabilitated."

Henry merely grunted. "That is for the king to decide. I must stay here. Come whenever you need me, but I want to be alone with my wife as much as possible. It seems…I have fallen in love with him."

Colin chuckled. "Seriously, Hal, are you just realizing this now?"

Surprised, Henry took his gaze off Kellen and looked at his old friend. "Is it that obvious?"

"To me, yes. You should have seen the look on your face when you tore off that wimple. You were gone at that very moment. I'm glad you've acknowledged it, because Kellen deserves your love. He is an amazing boy. We would never have been able to end this siege so easily if not for him."

"I know." Henry smiled for the first time since they'd left the camp. "I am the most fortunate of men."

"Make sure your wife knows that as soon as his eyes open." With that, Colin left.

Henry settled into his seat, his chin in his palm, eyes glued to his wife, looking for any signs of stirring. Hours had gone by when Kellen finally started to open his eyes.

Henry leaned forward. "Kellen, darling. Can you hear me?"

"Why shouldn't I? It's not like Isolde's arrow struck my ear." He started to sit up, grimaced and relaxed against the bed again before Henry could force him to. "How is she? And my father?"

"They both live."

Kellen heaved a sigh. "Good. I know I should hate them both, Isolda especially for trying to kill you. They're my family, though, and I can't help worrying about them."

"Of course. You have a kind heart. Here, it's time for more medicine."

Henry lifted Kellen's head up by cupping the back of his neck and helped him swallow what he judged to be about a spoonful of the cordial.

Kellen made a face. "It could taste worse, I guess."

"I understand exactly what you mean. I haven't forgotten how you forced it down my throat when I was stabbed." Henry rubbed the still-tender spot that remained bandaged. "We are quite a pair, are we not?"

His wife turned his head toward him. "The best possible kind." He licked his lips. "May I have some water?"

Henry jumped to his feet and raced to bring him a glassful. Once again, he helped the boy drink before laying his head down. This time, he carded his fingers through Kellen's hair to keep it from sticking to his face.

"Thank you." He looked away. "I must be keeping you from your duties. I'm sure there is a great deal to see to now that the castle has been taken."

"Yes, and all of it is in the capable hands of Colin and the others. There is no place I need or want to be other than beside my wife...who loves me." It was perhaps unfair of him to raise the subject so soon. He couldn't help himself.

Kellen scrunched up his face. "Did I say that?"

"You most certainly did." Henry sat on the chair again and took Kellen's hand to hold between his own. "It was before you passed out."

"I was in shock and didn't know what I was saying."

Henry's stomach dropped. "You didn't mean it? You don't love me?" When his wife didn't answer, Henry commanded, "Look at me."

Kellen complied, and there in his eyes Henry could see the worry.

His alarm subsided. "You're embarrassed, and you think I don't want to hear that from you, that I don't feel the same way."

"I don't expect you to. Our marriage was forced by circumstances, and..." Tears welled up in his pretty blue eyes.

"Don't cry, darling. It breaks my heart when you do, because I love you, too. I think I started to from the moment I saw that the nun in front of me was actually a beautiful young man."

Kellen sniffled. "I fear you are saying that only to please me because I'm injured."

Henry grinned. "I might if you were dying. You're not," he hastened to add. "Doctor Allen says you will make a full recovery, which is good because I want you to be mine for the rest of my life. You will believe me in this, wife," he added with mock sternness.

It had the desired effect. Kellen squeezed his hand. "I'm afraid you have no choice in the matter, my lord. I'm not going anywhere that you don't. And I promise I'll do my best to become the baroness you want and deserve."

"Oh, my darling Kellen, you already have."

Epilogue

Kellen frowned as he and Henry entered his boyhood chamber. "This isn't my room."

"Yes, it is." Henry kept his arm around Kellen's waist as he led him farther in and shut the door. "You should know your own way around this castle."

Kellen pointed at the bed. "This isn't mine." Then he swept his arm around the rest of the room. "None of the furniture is mine."

"In that, you are correct. I wasn't going to have you stay stuck with those pathetic pieces your miserly father had given you. You deserve finer things. And besides, your old bed was too small to accommodate the two of us."

A frisson of anticipation shot up Kellen's spine. It had been weeks since the siege had ended. His recuperation had been maddeningly slow, and naturally Henry hadn't touched him more than to give him a quick kiss. *Tonight, that changes.* He was more than ready for strenuous activities, and there was only one thing he wanted to spend his energy on.

He tugged on his husband's arm. "Come. Let's try it out."

Henry held his ground. "Not so fast, darling. I need to see for myself that you have recovered sufficiently for my attentions. I have a pent-up need for you, and I will not risk your health in venting it."

Kellen rolled his eyes, yet stayed still as Henry stripped him slowly of everything he wore. Soon he stood stark naked for his husband's inspection.

"You've seen me like this already, Henry. What do you hope to spot differently?"

Henry traced a fingertip lightly around the puckered skin that would fade but never go away, there to remind them both of what had happened.

A sudden worry occurred to him. "Do you find me ugly with this scar?"

"Silly boy. I hate it because it reminds me of how close you came to dying. It will never take away from your beauty, however, nor make me less eager to make love to you."

That word—love—had become a casual part of the words they spoke to one another. Kellen would never tire of hearing it. "I believe you, my lord husband. But you have me at a disadvantage. I want to see you, too, scars and all."

Henry hurried to comply, and the evidence of his own recent brush with death saddened Kellen. They had both survived, though, and their rising cocks were testament to that.

Kellen held out his arms. "Take me to bed."

Henry didn't hesitate to sweep him into his arms. He placed him with exquisite care onto a downy mattress that was more luxurious than his old one had ever been—and even better than what Henry had in his tent. Kellen felt pampered and special, particularly as Henry began to feast on his mouth while his hands roamed Kellen's body. He arched and shuddered as the man plucked each nipple, and the way his cock brushed up against his husband's was almost too much to bear. He feared he'd come too soon, and while history told him he would get aroused again quickly, he was beginning to enjoy the idea of waiting for his pleasure to mount.

Placing his hands between their bodies, he pushed his husband away. "I want a turn, Henry."

The man gazed down at him with blown pupils and a look of confusion. "A turn at what, darling?" He immediately swooped down to take Kellen in another kiss.

Kellen turned his face and pushed some more. "Let me play with you the way you do with me." He slithered out from under his husband, and taking Henry by the shoulders, tried to get him to lie on his back. It was like moving the mountain they now lived on. "Please, Henry. Let me *touch*. I want a chance to explore and give you pleasure for once."

Shooting a sly smile at him, Henry did as he'd been asked. He settled onto the mattress with arms spread. "I seem to recall waking up not too many nights ago with you sitting on my dick—a delightful way to be roused. So do with me what you will, wife."

Because he'd been thinking about this for a while as he'd convalesced, Kellen knew just what he wanted. He ran his fingers over his husband's face, admiring the high cheekbones and the square jawline. The man's hair had grown out a bit now that the siege had ended. It was surprisingly wavey, curling around his ears. His throat was thick like a bull's and his shoulders wide and strong. Skin was stretched tightly over corded muscle. He ran his hands over the mountainous biceps, marveling at how gentle the man was, given his great strength.

Every one was big and hard, such a wonderful contrast to Kellen's own slender frame. His husband could break him in two if he wished. He knew the man never would, choosing instead to protect him much as he served their king. Knowing how safe he was made Kellen even more aroused. And while every bit of his husband was intriguing, the thing that drew Kellen most of all was the hard, thick length of his cock. It bobbed against the treasure trail leading to it, and the big balls were tucked tight against his groin.

Kellen ran one fingertip down the length of the shaft. "I still can't believe something this big fits into me so well."

Henry grunted and bucked his hips. "It's a very impatient part of me, darling, I must confess. Your light touch is driving me mad."

Kellen tossed his head, happy to hear he had such an effect on his husband. "Well then, I should pay it better attention."

He had no idea what he was doing, other than through the memories of his husband doing it to him. Still, he figured Henry wouldn't mind his exploration too much. Straddling the man's legs, Kellen braced his hands on either side of his hips and bent over. He used only his tongue at first, tracing the path of his finger. That small effort made Henry groan. Emboldened, he played some more, tickling the cockhead and sliding his tongue through the slit. A tangy, salty taste hit his tongue. It was strange but not unpleasant, so he tried some more. When his husband murmured encouragement and bucked his hips, Kellen dared to take the tip into his mouth.

That small amount was enough to fill him. He used his tongue to play with it, but dared not try to take any more in. Henry was too big, and Kellen's mouth too small. Perhaps if he kept at it, he would manage to give a better blow job, although he couldn't imagine ever swallowing Henry's cock all the way down. He kept up his efforts, including his hand now to jerk the shaft. His entire focus narrowed down to this one spot. He squealed with surprise when Henry grabbed him by the waist and twisted him onto his back. The sudden movement caused him to scrape his teeth along the dick's taut skin.

Henry stared down at him with gleaming eyes. "I actually liked that—the bite of pain from your teeth. Obviously the rest of it was marvelous, as well, but we should consider adding in a little rougher play when you're up to it."

Kellen wasn't sure he understood what his husband was saying until he remembered the admonishment about taking off his helmet. "You mean like spanking?"

"Just so. Do you think you'd like that?"

Kellen didn't stop to consider. Instead, he bent his knees and lifted his legs, cupping the backs of his knees to hold himself in place. "Try it." He was mad to make the offer, yet his cock pulsed at the idea, and his hole clenched.

"Hmm. The angle would be better if you were on your hands and knees. But," he added before Kellen could change positions, "we mustn't put pressure on your wound. We'll make do for now."

Henry brought the flat of his hand against Kellen's ass with a light slap. The sensation was hardly what one could call pain, but it sent a shiver through him.

"More." Kellen closed his eyes and focused on that part of himself as his husband obeyed him.

Henry rained blows upon his ass in quick succession. Each one was a little harder than the next, and each time Henry's palm landed on his flesh, Kellen's arousal grew. He panted and writhed in an instinctive effort to avoid the strikes. His husband stayed the course, making sure to lavish his playful punishment on every part of Kellen's ass cheeks. The unexpected climax hit him just as hard as his husband's hands. Digging his fingers into the backs of his legs, Kellen gave unbridled voice to his pleasure. Here in the castle, with its thick walls, he finally felt free to hold nothing back.

When his cries died out into whimpers, Henry gave him a soft kiss.

"Well, I guess we've found something you like." He carded Kellen's hair back. "You are a marvel, darling. There is much of you for me to explore, and we have the rest of our lives to do so. For the moment, however, I really need to mount you."

Kellen could only nod. The bed dipped when Henry rolled off it and again when he returned. Kellen didn't have to look to know what the man was doing. And as much as he'd enjoyed playing with his husband, he loved having him command their lovemaking. It was a relief when his husband took control of his position, wedging his wide body between Kellen's legs and holding them up with his arms. He coated Kellen's hole with warm cream before sliding a couple of fingers inside.

Henry twisted his fingers. "You are so welcoming, darling. Look at how pliant you are, soft and relaxed, needing little preparation."

"Because I know now what you can do once your cock is inside me. I want you, Henry. I *need* you."

Henry thrusted deeply a few times before pulling his fingers all the way out. They were replaced within seconds by his husband's thick cock. It went in with silky smoothness, filling Kellen, stretching wide enough that one might worry he'd split open. But Kellen knew that wouldn't happen. Instead, his body came alive again, pleasure bombarding every nerve ending, his dick hardening quickly, despite his previous explosive orgasm.

Henry encircled one of his thighs with his arm and raised the leg even more. Then he clasped Kellen's cock and jerked it in time to his thrusts. And the way the man's pelvis brushed against Kellen's ass, tender from the spanking…it was too much. He came in a rush, with an arched back and a scream. He clawed at what every part of his husband he could reach. When the cock inside him swelled and warm cum splashed into his channel, he tugged Henry to him. They lay entangled, bathing each other in their harsh breaths. All Kellen could think of was that this was what he'd been waiting for his entire life.

* * * *

"It seems quite decadent to be sitting in bed, sipping wine and playing chess."

Henry smiled at his wife's innocent observation. It was his turn to move a piece, and he repositioned his rook before replying. "There are even more ways, if you want me to show you."

Kellen stared at the board, the hand holding his glass resting on one of his crossed knees. "Like what?"

Henry gave it some thought. "Like I can lick jam off your stomach...or your dick," he added with a wicked look that was designed to arouse. His wife was proving to be insatiable in bed.

Kellen made his move before narrowing his gaze at him. "Is that a thing?"

"Oh yes."

His wife waved his hand at his flaccid dick. "I think I'm going to need time to recover, my lord. You've worn me out. I may need a good night's sleep before I'm ready for more."

"Hmm. I like a challenge." So saying, he moved his queen. "Check."

Kellen sipped wine as he stared at the board. "You are a worthy opponent, Henry, in all ways." He took his gaze off the board. "What happens now?"

"I think I'm going to checkmate you in three more moves, darling."

Kellen grunted in exasperation. "I mean out there?" He gestured with his glass toward the door.

"I know." He'd hoped this discussion would be put off until the morning. He'd wanted one night free of the troubles in their world. His wife had other ideas, and that was okay. Whatever eased Kellen's mind was what Henry wanted. "Isolde is on her way to the king. Sir Robert is in charge of the escort."

Kellen dropped his gaze. "What do you think the king will do with her?"

"I'll wager his majesty is happy the siege and rebellion are over so quickly. There is an abbey far into the mountains where criminal noblewomen are sent by their families. I expect that will be your sister's fate, as that is what I've recommended to the king. She nearly killed you." The reminder still had the ability to turn his guts to water. He supposed it always would.

Kellen reached around the board to clasp Henry's hand. "She tried to kill *you*, husband. That, I cannot forgive." He rubbed his thumb along Henry's ring. It had been a happy day when they'd bought and exchanged rings once Kellen had recovered. "What about my father?"

"As you've seen, he's quite docile now that he doesn't have the support of his children, and his most loyal followers are either dead or transported to various regiments of the king. They will be closely watched and hopefully rehabilitated under the influence of far better leaders. Your father will remain the duke in name only, and he'll have the run of Highrock, so long as he behaves himself."

"And when he's gone?"

Henry realized where the questions were headed. "Did you know that your brother's widow was delivered of a son after she returned to her family?"

Kellen was clearly surprised. "No, I didn't know that. My father and sister were happy to see the back of her, and she, I imagine, was relieved to get out of Highrock. Brianna was always too nice for this place. If Wilfred knew about her pregnancy, he said nothing about it."

"I doubt he did. The timing of the birth implies she was newly so when he died. I've only received word of it since the siege ended. I didn't want to say anything about it while you convalesced." He paused before stating the obvious. "That child has as great a claim to the dukedom as you do. More really."

"He's welcome to it." Kellen tossed back the rest of his wine.

"Are you sure, darling? You could contest his claim. It's possible Lady Brianna gave birth to another man's child."

Kellen seemed to consider that before shaking his head. "No, I doubt she would do such a thing. She really was a kind and decent woman. Wilfred was hideous to her, but I can't imagine she would have dared to take a lover. I'm sure she has birthed my nephew, and he's next in line to the succession. I won't challenge him."

Raising their hands, Henry kissed the back of his wife's. "If you become the Duke of Cragmore, you'll outrank me." The thought of it rankled for some reason, which was a ridiculous reaction. His wife deserved the best that life could offer now, and he'd make a fine ruler of the North.

Kellen was silent for a moment, staring at the chessboard. "Every piece has its place." Laying his empty glass on the bed, he used his now-free hand to knock over his own king. Kellen stared at Henry. "Mine is by your side, as your baroness. I don't want to rule over anyone, Henry. You make me happy, no matter where we are, and I trust you to guide me through our lives."

With his heart stuttering, Henry swept away the chessboard, the pieces flying over the covers. His not-quite-empty glass spilled as well. He hardly noticed and didn't care, because all he wanted was to pull his wife into his arms. "I shall take good care of you,

Kellen. My love is something I don't have the words to describe."

Kellen curled into him. "Oh, Henry, I love you, too."

He ran his hand down the boy's silky back. "Then now is the best time for me to confess that we must stay here for the winter. The king has sent word that he expects me to act as regent until another can be appointed...if one ever is. The North is not an appealing place to many. I, myself, loathed the idea of coming here and waiting out your father's treason — until I saw you. That's when I learned that the North held the one thing I desired most of all."

"Oh, Henry." Kellen lifted his face for a kiss. "This place once held my worst nightmares. Now with you, it's the place of my dreams. Is there anything we can't accomplish if we are together?"

Henry hugged his wife tight. "No, darling wife, nothing at all."

Want to see more from this author? Here's a taster for you to enjoy!

Alien Blood Wars: Blood Dance
Samantha Cayto

Excerpt

Boston, Massachusetts
2017

Quinn blinked a few times to help adjust his vision to the dimness of the club. Compared to the bright, sunny day outside, the black walls, carpet and low-lit sconces gave the entryway a tunnel-like effect. The rapid eye movement caused his world to tilt a bit—or that might have been the gnawing hunger. He'd spent his last few dollars on a stale sandwich more than twenty-four hours ago and he was beginning to feel the drop in blood sugar. *God, if I don't get this job, I'm totally screwed.* He'd have to implement Plan B, and given that it meant selling his body on the street, he prayed that wouldn't happen.

The short hall led to a massive, two-story club room. For a second, Quinn stood and stared at the gorgeous opulence that was Lux, according to the sign on the door—a private gentlemen's club. The open floor plan contained a sunken dance floor surrounded by plush circular booths all along the edges. A shiny, dark wooden bar ran the length of the back wall and high-tops of the same material dotted the railings of the interior. Everything here was black, too, trimmed with silver and red.

What caught his attention the most, however, were the small, round stages at the four corners of the dance floor. Each one had a stripper pole imbedded in the middle. That was where he'd be working — *if* he got the job and *if* he didn't pass out from lack of food or an overload of adrenaline. *Why did I think coming to Boston would be a good idea?* He should have stayed in Michigan and found some low-paying work until he could afford to be bold. Right now, he felt like a lost kid in the big city. Thank God, he hadn't stopped in New York. The Big Apple would have eaten him alive in five seconds.

Instead of the two days that Beantown is threatening to take.

"Hey, kid, what's doing?"

Quinn jumped at the sudden question, issued in a booming voice to his left. Turning, he saw a huge man lounging at one of the plush tables against the wall. He had black hair in a Mohawk cut, pale skin and impressively large muscles bulging out of a tight, dark T-shirt. He had 'bouncer' written all over him, yet regarded Quinn with an appraising intelligence that made his empty belly quake even more.

The only thing breaking up the frightening façade was a red-headed twink curled in the guy's lap like a cat. The boy sported a half-shaved hairstyle where one side was stubble and the other had thick, straight strands curved against his jaw. Silver hoops twinkled around the shell of his ear. Quinn envied the edgy look and wondered if he could pull it off. That was, if he started making money, which wouldn't happen if he stood there with his mouth open.

Mustering the last of his courage, he answered, "An online ad said you were hiring go-go boys. I'm…ah, here to apply for the job." The fact that the club was advertising for boys, not girls, told him it was for gay patrons. The sight of the bouncer-guy with the twink confirmed it.

The hulk and his boy toy stared some more at Quinn. He tried not to shrink under the attention. He knew he had a scuzzy appearance, having traveled by bus for a couple of days and catching what sleep he could on a park bench the previous night. He'd at least gone to the nearby train station and washed in the men's room as best he could. He'd also put on the last of his clean jeans and a rumpled button-down that his grandmother had given him the previous Christmas — before he'd come out and turned into a wicked child undeserving of anything.

The man licked his lower lip. "How old are you?"

"Eighteen, sir." He knew he appeared younger and hoped that would earn him both a job and more tips. *God, it sucks counting on the world being populated by pervs in order to make a living.*

The man shot him a skeptical look. "You got ID.?"

"Yes, sir." Quinn walked to the table while he fished his wallet from his front pocket. He pulled out his driver's license and offered it.

The man reached over without having to move — his arm being that long — and plucked the plastic card from Quinn's trembling hand. He was so hungry and stressed that he felt like he was going to fly apart — or pass out. Face-planting on the thick carpet was a *definite* possibility.

"Relax, kid. I don't bite…much," the bouncer added with a flash of gleaming white teeth.

The redhead giggled and snuggled closer to the broad chest he curled against. Something predatory flashed in the boy's one visible eye. Quinn ignored it. He wouldn't mind putting up with some bitchiness if it meant earning a living without having to suck off strange men in alleys.

With a grunt, the man handed back the card. The action caused their fingers to touch and the bouncer's felt oddly cool. "Seems legit, although I'd swear you're no older than sixteen. I suppose the members will like that, though," he added with another blinding smile. "Go take him to the boss, Mackie."

The boy made a little mew with his pouty, full lips, but slipped off the man's lap, anyway. He looked incredibly slutty to Quinn, wearing a white sleeveless crop-top hanging off one shoulder and skinny jeans that hugged his thin body.

Cocking his hip, the boy raked his gaze up and down Quinn with his lips pursed. "You sure you can hack being a go-go boy? At a glance, I'd say you just got off the bus from get-me-the-fuck-out-of-here, Iowa, or something."

Quinn squared his shoulders. He wasn't going to let this kid get under his skin. "Close. It was Michigan, actually."

The twink opened his mouth and a yelp came out because the man had swatted his ass. "Be nice, Mackie, and do as you're told...or else."

Mackie gave a petulant sniff and glanced over his shoulder. "You'll punish me later?"

Jesus, the guy sounds eager for it.

The man gave him an indulgent smile. "Yeah, except it will be the kind you don't like."

"Humph." Mackie turned his gaze to Quinn. "Come on. Let's go see the boss. I suppose you'll be okay," he added with a flick of his wrist.

"Thank you, sir." Quinn gave the man a quick nod before falling into step beside Mackie.

They walked over to one end of the bar to a small elevator recessed into the wall.

Mackie pushed the call button. "Just an FYI, sweetheart, Val is all mine."

"Val?" The door swooshed open and they stepped inside.

Mackie pushed the top button for the fifth floor. "Yeah, the man I was recently and happily groping until you arrived. He's the head bouncer and the boss' right-hand man," he added with a flip of the long part of his hair. "They're also cousins or something. This is mostly a family-run business, except for a few outsiders like me. I've been here for over a year already," he added, as if proving his standing. "Val and I have been an exclusive item for most of that time. Neither of us is into sharing, either." He shot a warning at Quinn.

"Oh. No worries. I'm here for a job, not a boyfriend."

"Great, then we should get along famously."

The short ride caused sufficient movement to make Quinn lightheaded again. When they stepped into a small vestibule, he had to take a deep breath to steady himself. Mackie pushed a button on an intercom by a large door opposite the elevator. Like everything else in the place, the color scheme ran to black, red and silver and the lighting was muted.

"Yes?" A deep, rich voice floated out and right into Quinn's nervous system, causing goosebumps to rise on his arms and the back of his neck.

Mackie glanced up and following his gaze, Quinn saw a small camera mounted in the corner. "Val sent me for you to interview a dancer." The boy jerked his thumb in Quinn's direction.

There was no response for a few seconds, and once again, Quinn straightened his back to put on the best appearance. He could feel invisible eyes judging him. A clicking sound came from the door and Mackie twisted the handle to open it. Apparently, the boss was a man of few words.

The apartment they walked into followed the same décor as everything else. It was done in an open loft plan, yet it managed to convey a sense of coziness. *Probably the dim lighting.* Quinn felt as if he'd entered a cave—a lair, really—and its inhabitant didn't do anything to dispel that feeling as he strode toward them. Quinn's breath caught in his throat and his steps faltered.

If the bouncer, Val, had seemed big to him before, that was no longer true. While not as beefy, the boss gave the appearance of being at least taller and his shoulders were as broad as any linebacker. He had the same jet-black hair and pale skin as Val did, although he wore it swept back in a queue of unknown length. The style accentuated a sharp widow's peak. His untucked button-down shirt was a deep red, while his slacks were as black as his hair. He walked with a kind of grace powerful men often possessed and his amazingly violet eyes would have made Liz Taylor jealous.

The man stopped at the bottom of the three steps leading to a sunken living room and stuck one hand in a front pocket. "Who do we have here, Mackie?"

The boy shrugged. "Some kid from Minnesota who thinks he can dance."

"Michigan," Quinn corrected in a voice too hoarse to impress anyone.

Mackie shrugged again. "Same dif."

Because the other boy made no move to join the boss in the living room, Quinn planted himself in the entryway, too. He worked up some moisture for his dry mouth. "My name is Quinn Cooper, sir."

"Quinn," the man repeated, and this time, his voice held a hint of some kind of accent. "I'm Alexandru Stelalux. Everyone calls me Alex."

Okay, that explains the accent. He must be from somewhere in Europe. Quinn now had too much spit in his mouth, so he swallowed before speaking. "It's nice to meet you, sir. I hope you'll consider me for the job."

Mr. Stelalux—Alex—stared at him for a moment. His gaze made Val's perusal seem like a casual glance. "Do you have a resume?"

Quinn fixed his attention on his feet. "Um, no, sir. I'm sorry I didn't think of that. I've only ever worked at my family's hardware store, anyway. I have no dancing experience other than in school plays."

Mackie smirked at the confession and Alex chuckled, except it didn't sound like he was being contemptuous. "Well, that's all right. It's not like I'm considering you to tend bar or keep my accounting books. My clientele likes pretty boys to dance for their amusement. They don't even really care how skilled you are, either, so long as you look good doing it. The only real job requirement is having the right body."

He paced closer and cocked his head. "You've got a nice one from what I can see. All that shaggy blond hair and those bright blue eyes will certainly turn heads." He stepped to one side. "Yes, lovely profile. You'd make a nice contrast to the other boys. Don't you think so, Mackie?"

The other boy studied his nails. "I *suppose.*"

Alex's expression became stern. "Don't be bitchy, Mackie. You know I can't abide that."

Mackie straightened and appeared contrite. "Yes, sir." He slanted his gaze toward Quinn. "He's very pretty, and we haven't had a blond since Blake left."

"Exactly. Come here, please." Alex stepped back and flung himself on the end of a large sectional sofa. Then he braced his arms on the back of it, slung an ankle over a knee and watched as Quinn entered the living room area. "I'm afraid I'm going to have to ask you to strip. Nothing fancy, just take everything off except your underwear. We're not a nude club — not on the dance floor, anyway."

Quinn's head really began to swim and his palms turned sweaty. He told himself it was no big deal as he placed his scruffy backpack on the carpet by a chair. He would have to get used to being mostly naked in front of a big crowd. *If I can't do it now with only two guys watching, what hope do I have of keeping the job?*

Silent and self-conscious, he toed off his sneakers, pulled off his socks and unbuttoned his shirt. He folded the clothing and placed it on top of his pack before unsnapping his jeans. His vision blurred and he took deep breaths to keep oxygen pumping into his lungs. The sound of the zipper of his worn jeans lowering rang in his ears at an exaggerated decibel. As he slid the cotton down his legs, the room tilted enough that he grabbed the arm of the nearby chair to keep from tipping over. When he'd stripped to his boxer-briefs, he stood with his arms behind his back and his gaze fixed on the floor. His cheeks felt as though they were on fire.

"Hmm, a bit on the skinny side." A sigh crossed the room. "Then again, some patrons do like that sort of thing. I think you could use a few good meals, though."

The mention of food made Quinn's stomach grumble in protest before it clenched in pain. Quinn couldn't hold back the gasp. He wrapped his arm around his waist and listed to one side. Once more, he grabbed the arm of the chair, except this time, it wasn't going to be enough to keep him from falling. His vision blurred then closed to an ever-smaller circle of light before going completely black.

The last thing he was aware of was a rush of movement and something strong catching him.

About the Author

Samantha Cayto is a Boston-area native who practices as a business lawyer by day while writing erotic romance at night—the steamier the better. She likes to push the envelope when it comes to writing about passion and is delighted other women agree that guy-on-guy sex is the hottest ever.

She lives a typical suburban life with her husband, three kids and four dogs. Her children don't understand why they can't read what she writes, but her husband is always willing to lend her a hand—and anything else—when she needs to choreograph a scene.

Samantha loves to hear from readers. You can find her contact information, website details and author profile page at https://www.firstforromance.com/

PUBLISHING

Sign up for our newsletter and find out about all our
romance book releases, eBook sales and promotions,
sneak peeks and FREE romance books!

www.ingramcontent.com/pod-product-compliance
Lightning Source LLC
Chambersburg PA
CBHW050533260626
47157CB00004B/1589